THE WINTER
OF OUR
DISTEMPER

VICTOR CATANO

The Winter of Our Distemper
Red Adept Publishing, LLC
104 Bugenfield Court
Garner, NC 27529
http://RedAdeptPublishing.com/

First Print Edition: October 2019
Cover Art by Streetlight Graphics

This is a work of fiction. Names, characters, places, and incidents either are the product of the author's imagination or are used fictitiously, and any resemblance to locales, events, business establishments, or actual persons—living or dead—is entirely coincidental.

For Kim - the best and most supportive wife anyone could have

For Dany - my own personal Orson

For Mom - the first and longest fan of my writing

And mostly

For Dad

Victor Michael Catano

(1944-2019)

You taught me so much about perseverance, work ethic, kindness, and how to be a decent man.

I miss you every day.

ONE

"This is all your fault, Orson."

Sure, blame me. I'm the one suffering here. I have little legs.

"I told you not to eat that."

You shouldn't have left it out at eye level.

Sheila, my fiancée and Orson's owner, had kicked us out of the motel because Orson had decided to help himself to the McGriddles I had foolishly left on the coffee table for Sheila. That had made my usually charming and delightful fiancée very angry. She allowed herself one McGriddle a month and was none too happy about her dog stealing it. She banished Orson to the outdoors until she could compose herself. And since she wasn't about to walk him in the snow, that left me.

Orson and I trudged forward, and I tightened my collar to fight off the cold Maine wind. For the tenth time that morning, I thought about Florida.

Orson stopped to sniff at a tree, thought better of it, and walked away.

"What's wrong with that one?"

It's a dog thing, Gabriel. You wouldn't understand.

I suspected it was more of a way-to-annoy-the-person-walking-you thing than a dog thing. Ordinary bulldogs could be stubborn. Orson, however, was no ordinary bulldog.

It wasn't all Orson's fault. We had been living a transient life since finishing our business in Florida. Sheila, who was a witch, had parted ways with her coven, which also owned her apartment. So that meant

1

we'd effectively been evicted. That was five months ago. We'd also left a few enemies in our wake, and it was better not to stay in one spot.

At first, it was enormously fun. We were newly engaged, and it was a wonderful summer vacation. A different beach every week. A beautiful sunset every night. But as the months rolled on, the novelty wore off. We'd started talking about a place to settle down. We never discussed going to a frozen wasteland. I would have suggested somewhere warmer.

Sheila had always been strong, even for a witch, but the events in Florida had taken her to a new level. She was having a hard time controlling everything, so it was usually safest to do what she asked. When she told me to take Orson out into the howling wind and six inches of snow, I'd just put on mittens and grabbed a poop bag. And when she said to head north on I-95 to northern Maine, near the Canadian border, I'd done that too.

I had never been to Maine before. The Vacationland slogan on the license plates was mocking me. I assumed that Sheila had a reason to be here in January. I had to assume it, because she hadn't actually told me yet. I was pretty sure Orson knew, but he wasn't talking.

She has her reasons.

"Did she tell you what they were?"

Orson didn't answer. He sniffed a few dead leaves the wind had uncovered near the chain-link fence of the diner next to our motel. He got very interested in them.

I checked my watch. We'd been outside for about ten minutes. I hoped that was enough time for her to cool off, because I couldn't take much more cooling off on my end. "Is it safe to head back yet?"

Orson sniffed the leaves some more, deemed them okay to pee on, and did just that. *Mom says yes, as long as you have food for her.*

McDonald's was several blocks away, and the wind wasn't dying down. "Tell her that diner breakfast will have to do."

I ducked inside the diner and got us two more egg sandwiches, then we headed back to the room.

"If you eat these," I told Orson, "I'll leave you tied to a lamppost all day."

I'll tell Sarah McLachlan. She'll make a new commercial out of it.

Sometimes, I wished I couldn't hear Orson. Sometimes, I wished for a quieter animal. Like a bunny.

I like bunnies! They're fun to chase!

Sometimes. Like now.

A gust of wind dumped the snow off a nearby tree branch onto my head. I sighed and brushed it off my coat as we headed back to the room. Was it really only two days ago I'd been enjoying the warmth of Florida?

WE HAD BEEN VISITING our friend Wendy at her home in Lakeland. After our problems last summer, she was one of the few witches I trusted. Wendy had been a big help dealing with a bad couple of magical types who were after Sheila and Orson. She was also holding on to something important—a powerful souvenir of our encounter. It was a magical artifact, a large purple crystal that amplified and unlocked the powers of its user.

Wendy ran a sandwich shop near the baseball stadium. After a run-in with those same magic users, she'd had to rebuild her restaurant—all the way from the foundation. Since Sheila didn't trust any witch with it, Wendy had buried the crystal in the concrete she'd poured in the basement. The concrete also blunted the crystal's power. Somewhat.

We arrived just as she was closing up shop, so we all sat in the main part of the restaurant, sipping her excellent Cuban roast coffee.

"Any more problems from that bunch from last summer?" Sheila asked.

Wendy grinned mischievously, making her plump cheeks dimple. "No. I think you and Gabriel scared them very effectively."

"Blowing up a theme park around a guy's head tends to do that," I said.

Sheila looked out the new windows. The last time we were here, they'd been covered in duct tape and plywood. "The place looks great!"

Wendy nodded. "You get good service when the chief of police comes in at least once a week for your pastrami. No one wants to keep law enforcement from their food."

Orson was munching on a pile of said pastrami. *I understand the passion.*

We all laughed, then it got quiet. Sheila took another sip of coffee then asked, "So... has the crystal been giving you any problems?"

Wendy thought for a second. "No *problems*, really. It hasn't leapt out of the basement and commanded me to do its bidding. Still, there has been a lot more energy here."

"Good or bad?" Sheila had been worried the crystal was malevolent by nature. The last time she had touched it, she got furious because a witch had tried to kill me. She nearly destroyed half of Orlando.

Wendy shrugged. "Neutral. The air is just a lot more charged than it used to be. Business is good. Things are going well. I'm a pretty positive person. I think it picks up on that, on the emotions in the air."

Sheila relaxed into her chair. She rolled her neck as if working out a knot of stress. Her long black hair fell around her shoulders, distracting me. Then suddenly, she jolted upright as though she had been zapped with electricity.

I almost dropped my coffee. "What's wrong?"

Sheila didn't answer. She sat still and wide-eyed, staring between Wendy and me but not seeing us.

I looked at Wendy. "Do you think that's the stone?"

She shook her head. "That's never happened with me."

Orson whined. *I can't hear her.*

After a few seconds, Sheila snapped out of it. She shook her head then looked at me. "We need to go."

"What? We just got here. We've been driving all day." We had been taking a leisurely drive around the Gulf Coast and had just arrived from Mississippi.

"I don't care. We have to go now."

"What's wrong?"

"I can't tell you right now. We just need to leave."

Wendy looked concerned. "Is it the stone? Is it causing you problems?"

"No, not at all. It's not that. I just... I have to get somewhere."

Wendy nodded. She seemed to understand what was going on. I was glad someone did.

"Come back soon, okay? You three are always welcome."

Sheila gave her a big hug. "Thank you." Then she turned and walked outside.

Orson trundled after her. *Better hurry up, old man. She might try and hot-wire the car if you don't move it.*

I looked at Wendy. "What was that all about?"

She smiled and shrugged. "I can't say for sure, but it appears she got a message from someone. And you'd better hurry."

When the horn from the convertible blared outside, I gave Wendy a quick hug and hurried outside.

THE NEXT NIGHT, WE were in Maine. And not postcard Maine. Not Bar Harbor or Rockport. No, we'd taken 95 all the way from Florida up to the Canadian border then hung a left.

The drive from Florida to Maine would have taken twenty-six hours if we'd driven straight through, obeyed the speed limit, and didn't hit traffic. We did it in twenty-five. It would have been less, but both Orson and I refused to pee in a bottle.

Sheila was always nervous when I drove. She was a much more cautious driver, going slowly and letting people get in front of her. I was used to driving Humvees between the Green Zone and the airport in Iraq. She was always telling me to slow down and shouting, "Watch out for that car!" Said car was usually half a mile down the road.

Not today. It was the first time she'd told me to speed up.

"Can't you go faster?"

"This is a thirty-year-old vintage convertible. We're doing seventy-five."

"You didn't answer me."

"No, we can't. Really, it's great it's going this fast for this long."

Sheila went back to sulking and didn't say a word for another two hundred miles, when she complained about us stopping for gas.

Soon after that, when I got too exhausted to drive anymore, she took over. Sheila tried to prove me wrong and get the car past seventy-five. When we hit seventy-seven going downhill, she turned and said, "See?"

I had seen a few odd behaviors, being engaged to a witch with a psychic dog. I had never seen her like that, though. And all through the seventeen-hundred-mile drive, she'd barely said anything—especially about what was so urgent that we had to get to northern Maine right now.

We drove another hour before we finally hit Caribou at eleven o'clock at night. The sign on the way into town proclaimed it The Most Northeastern City in the United States. I'd been in barracks bigger than the town of Caribou.

We checked into the first open motel we found. Without even bothering to undress, Sheila fell onto the bed and was asleep in seconds. I took off her shoes and covered her with a blanket. I slipped in next to her, then Orson jumped up and curled up on my feet.

"Is she all right, buddy?"

Yes.

"Do you know what this is about?"

Yes. Maybe.

"Can you tell me?"

No. She'll tell you when she's ready.

I grumbled to myself.

I'm hungry. I want McDonald's.

"And I want to know why we're here."

Orson whined, but he went to sleep. I was out soon afterward.

TWO

I walked back into the motel room with our second breakfasts. The dingy stucco walls and the generic landscape painting didn't do a lot to cheer up the place. I hoped Sheila would be more relaxed. She smiled as she took the egg sandwich.

"I'm sorry I got so upset."

"It's okay. I should know better than to leave food out with Orson around."

Yes, you should.

I resisted the urge to kick some furry backside.

Sheila glared at her dog. "And you should know better than to take what doesn't belong to you."

Orson whined and gave her the sad-puppy eyes.

"No. That's not going to work this time."

Still whining, Orson slunk off to hide behind the bed while Sheila and I ate our sandwiches in silence. I turned on the TV. I didn't really care about college basketball highlights or frenetic game shows, but I just needed a little white noise to break up the silence. We chewed while letting *The Price Is Right* wash over us.

"Oh, fun! The Mountaineer game."

I had no idea Sheila was a fan, but at least she was talking. "Sure, but it's no Plinko."

"Plinko is random chance. Mountaineer requires skill."

"I guess you're right."

We were quiet again until the frat boy contestant sent the yodeler over the cliff because he had no idea what tampons cost.

Sheila smirked. "He hasn't had a relationship longer than a weekend."

I laughed at that. It was good to hear her make a joke. I decided to press my luck. "So, we're here…"

Sheila got quiet again.

"We drove straight through, and I'm still a little jittery from all of that awful gas station coffee I drank."

Sheila became very focused on the TV, staring intently at a cartoon general promising lower car insurance.

"You have to tell me. Why are we here?"

Sheila looked down and mumbled, "It's complicated."

"Oh, come on. Last summer, I went on a goose chase down the Eastern Seaboard, looking for you. I've been with you through the weirdest stuff I could ever imagine. I'm engaged to you. I've pledged to share my life with you. I can handle whatever you throw at me."

"I know. It's just hard for me to talk about this."

"What is it?"

She took a deep breath. "Gabe, there's a lot you don't know about me."

"Like your crush on Hugh Jackman? I'm cool with that."

She glared. "No. I'm serious."

"There is nothing, absolutely nothing, you could say that would make me stop loving you. What could be so bad?"

She just looked at me and didn't say anything for a few minutes. "We need to get going."

"Okay, I'll go check out." I hopped off the bed.

Sheila stopped me. "No, keep the room another day. At least."

"We're that close to… whatever it is you won't tell me about?"

"Yes."

I crossed my arms. "And you still aren't telling me."

"Not yet." She frowned in annoyance. I wasn't sure if I was the cause of it or not.

I suppressed a sigh. "All right."

We piled into the car and drove off, north and west on a two-lane road out of town. We hadn't gotten far when a familiar stink filled the air.

Sheila wrinkled her nose. "What is that smell?"

That awful tang, which somehow combined melting plastic and rotten fish, brought back so many memories. "It's pulp. There was a pulp and paper mill near us when I was a kid. It stank just like that. When the mill closed, half the town was out of work, but at least that stench was gone."

Sheila pulled her shirt up over her nose. "Oh, that's terrible!"

"I guess you get used to it. I never really did."

"I hope it's not like this the whole way."

"How far is that, anyway?"

"Not far at all," Sheila said, shifting uncomfortably. About ten miles farther, Sheila pointed to a narrow, rutted dirt road on the right. "There. Turn there."

I was glad she knew where we were going, because I would never have noticed it. I slowed to a near stop and took the turnoff.

The Galaxie bounced dangerously in the ruts. Twice, I had to steer hard to avoid sliding into the woods. Orson whined and took cover in the back seat.

After a mile, we pulled into a clearing. The midday sun beamed down on a quaint little cottage with pine walls stained dark brown and red trim around the windows. It looked like it had been designed to lure in Hansel and Gretel.

I stopped the car at the edge of the woods. "Is this it?"

Sheila nodded, and we got out of the car and stretched. The cottage was nestled on the far side of the clearing, up against the tree line. The pine smell in the air masked most of the pulp plant.

The door of the cottage opened. An older woman, tall and wiry with stringy gray hair, came out, wearing a floral dress with a mismatched floral shawl. When she saw us, she gave a whoop and ran toward us. The woman embraced Sheila in a bear hug that picked her up off the ground. "Sheila! You heard me! You came!"

Like an embarrassed teenager, Sheila tried to extricate herself from the hug. She finally gave up. "Hello, Auntie Mona."

THREE

Sheila barely spoke about her family. I knew her parents had been divorced and her mom was always suspicious of her abilities. The less said about her horrible, abusive stepfather, the better. But I never knew she had any other relatives, let alone ones who might be magical.

Mona finally released Sheila from her bear hug, but only because Orson barked for attention. She let Sheila go and started to coo over Orson while petting him a little too hard. Sheila caught her breath while Orson did his best to grin and bear it. He was much more tolerant once she found a cookie in one of the many pockets on her dress. Orson was easily bought.

She seemed nice, if a little overly affectionate. Still, if she lived out in the middle of nowhere, she probably didn't get many visitors, especially not family. She looked like an old hippie, but there were far worse branches to have on the family tree.

I wondered why Sheila wouldn't have told me about her. And if she was so embarrassed of Mona, why bring me at all?

Mona finally turned her attention to me. "And who is this young man? Is he the one I've heard so much about?"

"It depends," I said. "Was it good or bad?"

Mona hugged me and kissed my cheek. She smelled like fresh bread and green tea, which reminded me of Sheila. "Like you need to ask!"

"Let the poor man go, Mona." Sheila came to my rescue, but there was no humor in her voice.

"What—are you getting jealous?" Mona winked at me but loosened her grip. She turned to Sheila. "I'm so glad you're here! You came so quickly!"

"You made it seem like there wasn't much of a choice."

"True enough." She headed back to her door and waved at us to follow. "Come on, time's a-wasting. And I made scones!"

That was all Orson needed to hear. He ran inside after Mona, leaving Sheila and me to have a moment.

"So, now can you tell me what's going on?"

She sighed. "I will. This is just—" She turned to yell at the house. "We're coming! Give us a second!"

"Did I miss something?"

Sheila looked puzzled for a second then frowned, rubbing her hand across her eyes. "Right. You didn't hear that, did you?"

"No. But you sure did."

"Yeah, Mona can be like that. It is incredibly annoying."

"Like what?"

"Overbearing. Intrusive. Telepathic."

Sheila had always been able to talk to Orson, but she'd also been able to "hear" her mother when she was young. Soon after I'd learned about how she and Orson could chat with each other, she'd very patiently described how it worked: "When you get emotional, the thoughts just leap out at me. It's almost impossible for me not to hear them. Sometimes I can ignore them, but sometimes it's just too intense."

She had told me about this when the Eagles lost in the playoffs. They'd been favored to win, but they'd played like they had never actually touched a football before and had only read about the game on retranslated Japanese Wikipedia. She'd been in a coven circle two miles away, and she could feel my burst of anger. It was likely she could have felt that across state lines.

Usually, she could block out most of the background noise, but she was very in tune with close friends and family. "It's reassuring that even when things get rough," she'd told me once, "I can reach out and feel them close to me. Feel you close to me."

Whenever I asked her to guess what I was thinking, she would just roll her eyes and say she didn't need magic to figure *that* out.

If Sheila could get a mind jolt from Mona half a continent away, one that she couldn't ignore, that meant two things. Mona was as magically strong as Sheila. And if Sheila was that upset, something was very wrong.

FOUR

Inside, Mona's house was exactly what I'd expected—cramped and cluttered, yet comfortable and welcoming. The scent of bread I had smelled on her when she hugged me was almost overpowering in the house. A woodstove in the corner kept the room warm and comfy.

Sheila shifted awkwardly on the edge of an overstuffed couch. I sat back and sank deep into it. Getting up would be a problem.

Mona busied herself with collecting mugs, tea, sugar, and cream, which she piled onto a tray with a Bettie Page pinup printed on it. She hummed to herself while she worked, but I couldn't quite make out the tune. It was either "Für Elise" or "Crazy Train." To listen any more closely would inspire madness.

I tried to whisper to Sheila while Mona went back to get the scones. "So why wouldn't you tell me about Mona? She seems perfectly nice."

Sheila whispered back harshly, "You don't even know. This is how it starts. Every time. Hugs. Tea. Scones."

"Sounds terrible." I wriggled into the couch. "Don't forget the comfy chair."

She glared at me. "Not now. It always starts out in smiles and ends in screams. This is not the first time."

I wanted to ask more, but Mona had returned with the baked goods. "Here we are! Cranberry currant scones."

Orson sniffed the air. *What's a currant?*

Mona, Sheila, and I all started to answer at once. "It's like a raisin..."

Orson's head bobbed back and forth between us, with those big, sad eyes.

Mona threw her head back and laughed. "Well now! Isn't this one for the scrapbook?"

Sheila didn't find it all that funny. "Just stop it! Stop! I came all this way to deal with your emergency. Can you just drop the act and get on with it?"

The awkward, chilly pause that followed lasted so long that I felt like I could've walked into town and come back before anyone spoke.

Finally, Mona broke the silence. "Well, I'm sorry. I didn't think it would be such an imposition to come back and help your flesh and blood, the one who taught you about magic, in her time of need."

Sheila's neck and shoulders hunched up with stress. "No. You don't have to remind me. I already know I can't refuse you—and you know I hate it. Now tell me. Why did you call me here?"

Orson took advantage of the argument to steal a scone. *Oh, like little raisins. Only crunchier.* He crunched on the currants noisily.

Sheila glared at Mona. The soft lines around Mona's eyes sagged and wilted. I did my best not to look utterly confused.

Sheila got to her feet. "That's it. If you can't tell me what's going on, we're going."

I struggled to sit up, but the couch had me in its grip.

"All right. Enough dramatics." Mona sighed. "Please sit down, and I'll explain." She looked at Sheila for a few seconds.

Then Sheila shook her head and pointed at me. "No, Mona. Not like that. Gabriel needs to hear it as well."

"That just makes things so much slower."

Sheila glared at her. I'd seen that look. I knew better than to question it.

Mona narrowed her eyes. "Don't shout at me, dear!"

I hadn't heard anything, but Orson had covered his head with his paws.

Sheila wilted and sat down. "Please, for once, just get on with it."

"Very well." Mona smoothed out her dress and folded her hands in her lap. "It seems that I'm not a popular person in town these days."

Sheila didn't say anything, but she rolled her eyes.

"Yes, I knew you'd think that. But really, it's not my fault. I'm sure you smelled the new addition to town on the drive in."

I spoke up, since I finally had something to add. "You mean the pulp mill? Yeah, hard to miss."

"Yes, that." She crinkled her nose in distaste. "Northern Maine has a lot of things. Beautiful scenery, peace and quiet, wildlife, and especially trees. What they don't have is a lot of jobs. Especially after the recession hit a few years ago."

"I get it."

"Right. Too many trees and not enough work and a governor desperate to do some job-creating in an election year—and presto! An environmental nightmare gets plunked down in my backyard. And I tried to talk some sense into them, believe me!"

I could guess how well that must have gone over. Downtown Caribou was not exactly a thriving metropolis. The residents were probably more than happy to sacrifice a few pine trees to make their mortgage payments.

"But they didn't listen! They never do! They weren't even going to let me speak! They stacked the town meetings with pro-business speakers and wouldn't let anyone else near the microphone. I tried to say something, just make a few points about how they were being short-sighted, but I got shouted down! I got dragged out of the town hall! They arrested me for causing a public disturbance! As if constitutional rights are a nuisance!"

Sheila finally spoke up. "They arrested you? Why didn't you call me then?"

"Oh my, it hardly seemed important. It was four years ago. I've spent many nights in jail for fighting the good fight. And I was quite prepared to spend one more. Anyway, the fix was in. The governor was a state senator in this district. He made 'economic development' in the more rural parts of the state a big priority. They weren't about to let some old hippie stop that train."

I piped up. "I'm guessing that you were probably the only one in town who was more concerned about the environment than jobs."

Mona smiled at me. "Now, that's where you're wrong. While I was certainly the most... vocal opponent of the pulp mill, I wasn't the only one."

She paused to take a sip of tea. "I had barely sat down on the bench in the cell when the police came to let me out. I figured they'd made their point and were ready to let me go with a warning, but no. It turned out that two youngsters had bailed me out. I took them for college kids. Environmentalists, doing the old hippie a favor for speaking out."

"There's a college nearby?" I was surprised. From what I'd seen, the town didn't seem big enough to support a one-room schoolhouse, let alone a college full of young people.

"Oh sure! Presque Isle has a big environmental studies program. One of the professors tried to speak about the carbon footprint the plant would leave, but he didn't get near the mic, either."

Sheila frowned and angrily splashed a sugar cube into her teacup. "I'll bet *he* didn't get arrested."

Mona ignored that. "There was one boy and one girl. They both had on jeans and hemp hoodies. They thanked me for trying to speak up and asked if I would join them for coffee. I couldn't really say no. They put up a hundred dollars in bail. We went to the diner. We walked over, and they kept talking about nature and the earth and the environment and how humanity was stampeding toward extinction. Nothing out of the ordinary."

I grinned to myself. I didn't have to look at Sheila to picture her biting her tongue hard enough to leave a dent.

"I was expecting the professor to join us. I thought he'd probably given them the cash to bail me out and stayed at the meeting to try and voice his concerns. But someone else was already waiting at the table. He looked very friendly, but also very... intense. He was middle-aged. His hair was a bit long and shaggy. It was dark brown but graying in spots. He had a gentle face, with laugh lines and crow's feet, but those eyes. Bright and dark—almost black. He shook my hand, and I got such a chill. I could tell he was going to be trouble."

I looked at Sheila. We'd both had our share of people like that. Unfortunately, we didn't always get the chance to walk away.

"We sat down. He introduced himself as Caleb, and he started in right away. About how the planet was in danger and how we had to take the right steps to save it. Now, I've been talking about that since the seventies. I said it was good to meet some like-minded people. He said I didn't know just how like-minded we were."

Mona took a sip of her tea, and when she continued, she was much quieter. "That's when I felt them in here." She pointed to her head. "All three of them. I heard him. He said, 'See? Very like-minded.'"

That was a little hard to process. "I always thought that people like you were... uncommon."

Mona chuckled. "We certainly are! I've met more honest politicians than telepaths, and to be at a table with three others... Well, I thought that must be the entire population of New England."

Sheila looked genuinely concerned for the first time, like there might actually be something to the situation. "Three people? At once? That must have been terrible!"

Mona frowned. "It wasn't pleasant. I could barely hear the kids, but they were with him. And he was clear as day. He was trying to flex, show me how strong he was. He told me—well, *thought*—that there were more of us, more people who cared about nature and didn't like what was happening. He wanted me to join them."

"Wait," I said. "How did he even know about you?"

Mona chomped on a bit of scone. "I'm not exactly a fainting flower."

"No, I get that. How did he know you were magical?"

Mona shrugged. "I don't advertise it, but I don't keep it a secret. I'm sure people whisper things. After that one Halloween, I think I officially became local color."

I still wasn't sold. "But it's a small town, and you'd never seen this guy before. Where did he come from?"

"It's not that small. Word gets around. I considered joining up with them to fight the mill. Strength in numbers and all. But those eyes. The way his voice sounded in my head... I thanked them for bailing me out and for the coffee. I offered to pay them back, but he wouldn't hear of it. 'Just think about what we talked about. We have real power. We can do things to stop them. We can always use your help.' He said I would come around."

That all sounded pretty creepy.

Mona looked at me. "You got that right."

Sheila jumped in. "So, then what? They just let you walk away?"

"Sure. I was creeped out but not too worried. I can handle myself. A few months went by, but I didn't hear anything. The mill was approved, of course, and there was a big groundbreaking ceremony. And that's when things got bad."

She hopped up and pulled a scrapbook off a crowded shelf. She opened it up to the front page from the local paper. The headline blared "Bizarre Protest Disrupts Groundbreaking." The photo showed a blurry image of several figures dressed in animal hide and loincloths and not a lot else. One wore antlers.

"It was the man from the diner. Caleb. He showed up just as the governor took the stage to do his usual bit about jobs and Maine being open for business." She peered down at the paper as if she were about to read from the story then looked up at us. "You know, it would be easier just to show you."

Sheila started to protest, but before we could react, Mona grabbed our hands. She closed her eyes, and we were transported to the cold spring day. Snow was still ankle deep on the ground. The calendar may have said spring, but it was still well below freezing.

A pudgy man I assumed was the governor hopped off a low stage and walked to a patch of land that had been hastily cleared of snow. He shook hands with another man in a barn coat and a hard hat. Probably the company head. A few reporters readied their cameras as the men each took a shovel and prepared to stick it in the hard ground.

"Stop this blasphemy!" a voice boomed out. It was loud and clear and seemed to come from all around us.

Someone in the crowd pointed, and we turned to see a man in a loincloth. It was long, almost to the ground. He had some kind of wrap made of hide draped around his arms and shoulders. His crown of antlers poked two feet above his already-imposing height. It had to be Caleb. Others appeared at different points around the clearing, stepping forward from the trees. They were all dressed like Caleb, minus the horns, except for two women who weren't concerned about the cold or their modesty.

"We have tried to warn you. We have tried to get you to stop this disrespect to Kisulk. We have tried to reason with you. We are finished. If you will not listen to reason, we will use force to make you respect Kisulk." The leader's voice echoed across the clearing, sounding much louder than should have been possible.

A low rumble started in the clearing, followed shortly by tremors. It seemed to start from the groundbreaking patch. After a few seconds, the tremors became violent enough that several people stumbled and fell. It didn't seem to reach the tree line where the strangers in loincloths stood and watched. The governor fell on his back, and a crack opened up in the ground next to him.

Then all was still. The earth stopped moving. The crack in the ground stopped just shy of the governor's head.

Caleb spoke again. "Heed this warning."

The lot of them faded away into the trees.

After a second, the governor started cursing and yelling at his detail of state troopers. They ran into the woods, along with the local cops.

The governor attempted to salvage the situation by grabbing the microphone and trying to calm the crowd. "It's okay, folks! Look, he helped break open the ground for us!"

The crowd wasn't convinced, though. Dozens of eyes turned toward me, and I felt the suspicion, fear, and distrust. Even if Mona wasn't hearing them telepathically, the hatred in their eyes was practically shouting, "It's her. She didn't want this plant. She must have something to do with it."

Mona let go, and I was back in her cottage with her and Sheila.

Sheila was pissed. "Don't do that again!"

"Sorry. It just seemed more efficient to show you what I saw."

"More efficient for you."

I was more than a little confused. "What did he say? 'Kisulk'? What is that?"

Mona was happy to get away from Sheila's glare. "It's the native creator spirit in tribes of the area. I looked it up once he started going on about it back at the diner."

"You didn't mention that before!" Clearly annoyed, Sheila crossed her arms.

"I didn't think it was important at the time. Most of my friends in the seventies talked about Mother Earth and Gaia and things like that. Kisulk is the creator of Earth in the native traditions. It didn't seem too odd that local environmental activists would latch on to that."

"Are they all Native American?" I asked. "The loincloths were a bit much."

Mona shrugged. "It's hard to say. I knew a lot of blond, blue-eyed trust funders back in the day who claimed their great-grandmothers were Cherokee princesses or some nonsense like that. He didn't look like it when I met him—and his college student friends certainly didn't. They may have distant relatives. But I'd have to say no."

I thought about what I'd seen at the end, when the town turned on Mona. "And then because you were such a vocal protester and because you were at the groundbreaking, people assumed you had something to do with that."

Mona nodded. "That's right. They... tolerated my eccentricities before. After that, I was shunned. I could barely get served in any store in town. I have to drive an hour south just to get milk. Everything else, I get on Amazon."

"So, Caleb and company threatened everyone, and you got blamed for it." Clever. Not nice but clever. "Were there any more incidents?"

Mona laughed bitterly and passed over the thick scrapbook. It was filled with newspaper clippings about accidents and sabotage at the construction site. Someone stole all the porta-potties. All the tires on the construction vehicles were flat one day. Holes that had been dug on Monday were refilled by Tuesday. Company security guards and state troopers were on-site around the clock. Nothing seemed to work.

Animals seemed to act crazy around the site as well. One day, a moose got through the gate and chased away the workers. An army of raccoons swarmed the coffee truck and stole all the food. The next month, it seemed that every bird in Maine had migrated north to shit on the workers.

Any one of those on its own would have been weird—an odd story for the local news to cover. Together, and read back-to-back, it seemed obvious that something was at work.

"And it was always the same. Something would happen, and the police would pay me a visit. They had no evidence! Really, did they expect to find fifteen porta-potties in my backyard? A how-to-train-your-moose handbook? They would always give me a warning and tell me to watch myself. And I was watching, just not for what they thought."

From a drawer in the coffee table, she produced a letter written in simple block print. *There's still time to join us and be on the right side.*

"It's from him. They started coming soon after the groundbreaking." She pulled a thick folder off the shelf. "They haven't stopped. And they get less friendly."

"Less friendly" was an understatement. They started off with polite urgings to "please reconsider" and devolved into final warnings and a "you better watch out!" I hadn't seen threats like that since I'd been behind on my credit cards.

"But why do they care about you so much?" I asked. "They seem to be making plenty of trouble without you."

"Well, yes and no. They certainly were a huge pain in the ass, but as you can tell..." Mona paused to sniff the air. "They only succeeded in some delays and cost overruns. The plant finally opened last fall, just in time for the governor to start his reelection campaign."

"So, if the plant is open, why keep this up?"

Mona chuckled. "Dear, you don't understand how movements work! Just because the plant opened, it doesn't mean the protests end. If anything, that's when you can step it up because the evidence of pollution and corruption is even more overpowering!"

"Protests? You seem to know a lot about it."

Mona sighed. "That may be the problem. I think my reputation may have preceded me with this particular group of environmental defenders. You see, when I was younger, I—"

Sheila jumped in, cutting Mona off with a sharp wave of her hand. "We're not getting into that. Not now."

I was shocked by Sheila's anger. I wanted to ask what was wrong, but I knew when to keep my mouth shut.

"You still haven't told us what you want," Sheila continued. "I'm sorry the townspeople think you're crazy enough to slash tires and send raccoon armies after them, and I'm sorry this Caleb guy thinks you should be besties, but I don't understand what you expect us to do about it."

Mona sighed. "Isn't it obvious? I want to be left alone. I want the townspeople not to fear me. I want things to go back like they were a few years ago."

"So, learn to talk about the environment without getting arrested. That might be a start."

Mona ignored the bait. "Mostly, I need you to stop this." She fished an envelope out of her skirt pocket. It had her name written on it but no stamp or return address. "This came two days ago. I saw it, and I called for you at once."

Sheila unfolded the letter and let out a small gasp. She passed it to me.

It was the same block print as the first letter, and the message was plain and simple.

Join us or leave. The pestilence upon our land will be a smoking crater by week's end.

"They're going to blow up the mill." Mona exhaled this statement in one quiet breath as she looked down at the floor. "And the police would never believe I had nothing to do with it, if they even listened to me before they threw me in jail."

FIVE

Sheila assured Mona that we would do what we could, then we headed back to the motel. Orson whined in the back seat while Sheila stared out the side window into the darkness. The sun set around four in the afternoon up here.

"Is it always like that with you two?" I asked while trying to navigate the ruts in the dark and not having much luck at it.

Sheila sighed. "Pretty much. She's the same as ever. Everyone's always out to get her. Environmental mania."

"No, that thing about her reputation preceding her. You cut her off. What was that about, and why didn't you want to get into it?"

Sheila leaned back in the seat and crossed her arms. "I really don't want to talk about it."

The car hit a big pothole so hard that it jolted me forward. Orson yelped in the back seat as he slid onto the floor. I'd officially had it—with both the road and with not getting a straight answer. "Well, that's too bad, because we are going to talk about it. Starting now."

"Stop!"

"No, I will not stop. I need to know why you don't want to talk about her even though you dragged us cross-country to get here."

Stop the car! Orson barked frantically.

I slammed on the brakes, trying hard not to slew into the ditch, right as a dim outline appeared in the road ahead, just beyond the headlights' reach. It was huge and blocked the road. The moon broke through the clouds, illuminating the dark shape. It was a moose that stood about eight feet high. Steam rose off its fur and billowed from its nose. Its curved antlers were enormous, at least six feet wide and showing a number of points.

"Shit! Sorry." I exhaled and waited for the moose to move on out of the path, but the moose didn't seem to have any interest in moving. "So, do I honk? Or do I just wait it out?"

Heck if I know.

"You're a big help."

I recalled a hunter telling me once that he'd hit a moose with his car. He'd hit the moose in its thin little legs, and one thousand pounds of body fell onto the hood and engine, totaling the car. The antlers had ended up in the driver's lap.

I had no idea if honking the horn would scare it off or sound like a challenge. I didn't want to risk it, and I wasn't in a big hurry. I could wait. The moose, however, could not. It turned to face us. The moon might have been playing tricks, but I could have sworn its eyes were glowing red. Then the moose lowered its head and charged straight at us.

"Oh, shit."

Sheila screamed. Orson barked. I slammed the car in reverse and tried to back up as fast as I could—which wasn't all that fast. The car bounced across the ruts, and I hit my head on the soft roof. In the rearview mirror, I saw Orson go airborne.

The moose was almost on top of us. I tried to go faster. Bounce, bounce, bounce. He lowered his head, and the antlers almost speared the hood of the car. I floored the gas, and we gained some ground.

Then the car hit a crater in the road. Something snapped, and the car lurched to the right, facing into the woods. I tried to rock the car into drive and back to reverse, but the tires were stuck. The car had either bottomed out or broken an axle—or both. We were dead in the water... or possibly dead in the road.

"Sheila, grab Orson and run back to Mona's house!" I tried to keep the panic out of my voice.

"No!"

"Do it. I'll distract the moose with the horn."

"There isn't time!"

She was right, the moose was only a few yards away. And kept charging.

"Sheila, get out!" I pleaded.

She ignored me and grabbed Orson by the collar. Their eyes sparked golden as Sheila swept her hand through the air. A tree fell on the road, just in front of the moose as it thundered forward. Startled, the moose bellowed and skidded to a stop. It looked around, almost as if it were confused as to why it was there, then it walked slowly into the woods without giving us a second look.

It took a few seconds for me to catch my breath. "Are you all right?" I asked.

Sheila looked at me. "Yes, hero man. We're fine."

Sometimes I forgot what it meant to date a witch. It did have its advantages. "Sorry. I just reacted without thinking."

Sheila exhaled. "I didn't think, either. That moose scared me. If you hadn't reacted, I wouldn't have had time to do anything."

I got out of the car to check on the damage. Both the rear wheels were canted at awkward angles. I was no mechanic, but it looked like an axle or the tie rod ends—maybe both—was broken. I stifled a groan. That meant a lot of money and a lot more time in Caribou, more than I wanted to spend on either one.

So what was that about?

Sheila scratched Orson's neck. "Sorry, baby. I'm not sure."

Then I remembered a tidbit from Mona's story. "Mona mentioned something about a moose going crazy on the construction site."

Sheila sighed. "You don't think that Caleb person did this? I have a hard time trusting Mona on just about anything."

"It just seems odd. I didn't think moose generally attacked people."

"I don't know. There's so much about Mona that I try not to think about."

I put my arm around Sheila and hugged her close. I tried not to think too hard about how I'd been enjoying a nice sandwich in Florida two days ago rather than dealing with homicidal moose. I gave Sheila a quick kiss and clambered out of the car to go get a tow truck.

SIX

I trudged back to Mona's house, keeping an eye out for murderous moose and strangers wearing loincloths. Sheila, having preferred not to deal with her aunt any more that evening, waited in the car.

Mona met me at the door, since—of course—she knew I was coming. And of course, she insisted that Caleb was behind the moose attack. "Moose just don't attack people! He must have been provoked!"

I didn't feel like arguing. "Can I borrow your phone? We're going to need help getting out."

Mona nodded vigorously. "Of course, sweetie. You can use my Triple A if you need to!" We threaded around her sofa and her crammed bookcases to the kitchen, where a big black box with a round dial was mounted on the wall. *Of course Mona would have a rotary phone.*

I had to wait for the voice mail menu to cycle through. But once I spoke to someone, I was told a driver would be there in less than an hour. I slogged my way up to the turnoff from the main road to wait, because there was no way the driver would see it in the dark.

Ninety minutes later, a dingy red tow truck finally chugged up. As soon as he saw me waving, he pulled over. When he realized where we were, he turned white and almost drove away. If I hadn't jumped right in front of him, he would have left us there.

"Hey! Where do you think you're going?"

He stammered and tried to give a sheepish apology. "Uh, sorry! I have the wrong address. I gotta go."

"King Towing? Call 237? No, you're in the right spot."

"Oh... Uh, I can't go down there. Private road, so, uh... I'll just be..."

Oh good, he was part of the Great Caribou Shunning of Mona. I slammed my hands down on the hood of the truck. I glanced at the name tag on his overalls. "Look, Jimmy, we went down that road to turn around, and a moose jumped out at us. We swerved and got stuck in a ditch. My pregnant wife is down there, terrified, and you are not going to leave her in the cold!" Some of that was kind of true.

That got him flustered. He gulped hard. "Look, I'm sorry, but..." He seemed to be dazed for a minute then shook his head. "Yeah, of course, sorry... I'll back down the road, just guide me, okay?"

I took my hands off the hood of the truck as he started it up. He swung the truck around to the edge of the drive then smiled at me as I got behind him to guide him down the dark path. I could have sworn he was whistling from the front seat as he bounced along.

It took a few minutes to ease the tow truck over the ruts and bumps in the dark. When we finally made it back to the Galaxie, Sheila had leaned back to take a nap. Orson was protecting her by snoring and drooling on her lap.

After a lot of scooting around, the tow truck was finally lined up with the front of our car. The driver hooked up the winch and dragged it slowly onto the flatbed. As the car leveled out, he gave the undercarriage a quick look.

"Yeah, looks like an axle, all right. I'll take you back to the garage, but they won't be able to get to it until the morning. You want to ride up front?"

"No, we'll be okay in here."

He nodded and climbed in the cab of his truck. I got in our car next to Sheila, and he hauled us away. Sheila awakened from her nap.

"Was that you?" I asked. "He almost drove off when he saw whose house that was."

"What, you mean me? Your terrified, pregnant wife?" She grinned.

The tow truck lurched forward. I watched the dark road fall away behind us. No moose popped out. "Can we talk about this now? We're going to be stuck here at least another day or two until they fix the car."

Sheila sighed. "Soon. I promise. Let's just get a little distance from here."

The car jumped again as the tow truck pulled us off the dirt and onto the paved road. We put some miles between us and Mona, but I knew from experience that distance from family was always hard to judge.

AN HOUR LATER, WE WERE back at the motel. The tow truck driver had been nice enough to give us a ride—once Sheila suggested it to him. I didn't care how it happened. I had no desire to walk in the cold anymore.

"Sweetie," Sheila said, "Orson needs to go out."

Yay.

I heard that. I'll just use your shoes next time.

"You know, it's getting tiresome with everyone in my head."

"Sorry, honey."

As long as I get a walk.

Ah, man's best friend. I went with him outside, leash in hand.

Orson sniffed a lot of things.

"Any news?"

This hot poodle bitch is pregnant.

"Should I buy cigars?"

Ha, ha. Not the father.

"You sure? Is there a doggy Maury show we can get you on?"

Orson growled his displeasure while he peed.

FINALLY, WE GOT BACK to the room. Sheila was propped up in bed, watching a gossip show. She looked wrung out and annoyed, although I didn't think the misbehaving movie stars were the source of her irritation.

"Let me guess," I said. "Some starlet got out of a limo with no panties, some teen singer said something racist on Twitter and made a half-assed apology, and some teen heartthrob either drove drunk or got into a fight."

"Three for three. Now who's a mind reader?"

I kicked off my shoes and sat down next to her. "Good, 'cause there's something else on my mind."

She winked at me. "That's always on your mind."

"Come on, don't play innocent. You know what I mean."

Sheila sighed.

Now I was really starting to get annoyed. "Enough of this. What's the story with you and Mona?"

Sheila closed her eyes and rubbed her forehead. After a few seconds, she looked up at me and took a breath. "Did you ever hear of Three Mile Island?"

"Yeah, of course."

"Well, that was Mona."

I must not have heard that right, since that seemed insane. "What?"

"Mona caused the Three Mile Island disaster."

I knew a guy from England once. He had some wonderful phrases and slang, of which one of my favorites was *gobsmacked*. It meant to be stunned speechless, like a person might feel after being smacked right in the face by something.

I was gobsmacked.

My eyes popped open in disbelief. "You're telling me," I sputtered, "that the biggest nuclear accident in this country's history—the closest we ever came to a full meltdown—that was all her?"

"Yeah."

I waited for her to go on, but she didn't. "I'm guessing there's a little more to it?"

"Thirty-five years ago, she wasn't quite the harmless old hippie she looks like now. She was fresh out of college, head filled with idealism. And a lot of that was focused on the environment."

"A nuclear meltdown seems pretty environmentally *un*friendly."

"You heard her talk about the pulp mill. Just because the project's done doesn't mean the protests stop. That's when you have to step it up."

This was crazy. Suddenly, I couldn't sit still. Feeling antsy, I got up and paced the small motel room. "How did it happen? I never heard about any kind of activism or terrorism causing it. I always heard human error or equipment breakdown."

Sheila nodded. "Believe me, I did some research about it. The official reports blamed a stuck valve in the cooling system, and the operators either didn't see the warning lights or misinterpreted the readouts. It wasn't until the second shift came in that they realized what was going on, and by then, it was too late."

"So how did Mona..." I slumped into the tiny armchair by the little table. I knew how.

Sheila smiled grimly and tapped the side of her head. "Yeah. You got it. She was dating one of the reactor technicians. Poor sap named Everett. Once they were close, she could pretty much get into his head at will. So one night, Everett sees the valve indicator isn't working right and starts to panic. Mona tells him to ignore it. Again and again and again."

Sheila clenched her fist. From across the bed, I could feel the little half-moon marks her nails were making on her palm. "A full meltdown would have been a catastrophe! That plant's a hundred miles from Philadelphia! Thank goodness there were enough fail-safes that it was only a partial disaster."

"How did you find out about this? Did she tell you?"

Sheila frowned. "Not straight out. When I was young, she came to stay with my mom after the divorce. She stayed for about a year. She helped out around the house and took care of me when Mom had to work. Mom mentioned how I spooked her by seeming to know what was on her mind before she said it. That got Mona's attention."

Her eyes got moist. "It was hard when I started getting my magic. I was just a little girl, and everything seemed to be talking to me. It was terrifying. Mom didn't know what to do; she was scared of me. But Mona... she believed me. She knew what was going on. She helped me focus so I didn't hear every weird thought from people around me. We were very close. We had to be—we could share everything! There was such a bond. But that became a problem."

Of course. They shared *everything*. Her fist was still clenched tight. I moved over to the bed and sat beside her. I took her hand and massaged it until she relaxed a bit.

Sheila put her hand over mine. "I was maybe ten. One day, I came home early from school, and she didn't feel me coming. She could usually say hello to me a block away. She must have been waking up from a nap. And I felt the pictures in my head. I saw the cooling towers. I felt the panic. And I felt her laughter. I saw it in my head. I saw the plant workers freaking out and lights flashing, and I saw her being happy about it. I knew what a meltdown was. I had seen that *Day After* movie on TV, and it scared the pee out of me. I was appalled. I asked her why she was so happy about the plant accident. She told me I would understand when I was older."

"It doesn't sound like something to be proud of."

"You'd think so. But that accident caused a major shift away from nuclear power. You know that *China Syndrome* came out like two weeks before that happened? You couldn't ask for better timing. There have been no new nuclear plants since then. So for a certain type of protester and a certain type of magical person, she has a lot of notoriety. The witch that stopped nuclear power."

No wonder Caleb was so excited to have her on his side. A powerful witch who would do anything to protect the environment was a huge asset. "So, if she was so pumped to nuke Pennsylvania, why would she care about a pulp mill in northern Maine?"

Sheila shrugged. "It's a good question. I wonder if she'll tell us." She gave a short bark of a laugh. "Who knows? Maybe she's changed." She laughed some more. "Not long after that, Mona left. Mom was pretty much back on her feet, but she said Mona was welcome to stay as long as she wanted. I think she was relieved that there was someone I could talk to. It put less pressure on her. But Mona said she had to get going, that she'd imposed long enough. But I knew why she left. It was because I knew about what she'd done."

Sheila sighed. "After that, I would hear her every now and then. When I got really upset, I could feel her calming me down. When my mom and stepdad got married, I heard her almost every night. Not long after that, I found Mr. Whiskers."

Mr. Whiskers was her first familiar. He had hated every living thing on this planet except Sheila. He'd been old and sick when I met him, and both Orson and I had scars to remember him by. "You think Mona sent him?"

Sheila shrugged. "Possibly. Familiar magic is a little hazy at times. They're supposed to find you, but nothing says they can't get a little push."

"Meltdown aside, it sounds like Mona tried to look out for you."

"Only to a point. She helped me out a lot when I was young, but it's been all the other way since then. Every time she gets in trouble, she needs me to bail her out. This is not the first time I've had to come running, although it is the most urgent call she's given me."

"So why come back?" I asked. "She helped you out when you were a kid, but you must've paid her back by now."

She shook her head sadly. "It's more complicated than that. That year she was with us, she was more of a mother to me than Mom was. If she hadn't been there to help guide me, I don't know what I would've done. Or what Mom would've done. She was a single mother with a deadbeat ex and had to work two jobs to keep us in a crappy apartment. It would have been a challenge to raise a normal kid, but a daughter who knows when you're fibbing to her about why Dad hasn't called in a month?" She paused and sighed deeply. "If Mona hadn't been there for me, I wouldn't be who I am today. I might not even be here right now. I owe her a lot. And as much as she frustrates me and angers me, I just can't say no and walk away."

"Did she do any other environmental actions?" I stopped. "Wait, she never went to Russia, did she?"

"As far as I know, Chernobyl can still be blamed on human error and Soviet technology. But yeah, she could always be found chained to a redwood or something."

It was a little hard to reconcile the nice hippie lady who made scones with a woman who would have laughed while a mushroom cloud engulfed Philadelphia. "So what changed? Why is she hiding the past instead of embracing it?"

Sheila shook her head. "I don't know. She was never shy about it before. She always told me to embrace my nature and never apologize for what I believe in." She paused to stroke Orson, who was lying next to her on the bed. "Mona was everything to me. It was such a relief to know that I wasn't a complete freak. I felt so alone when I was a kid! Hearing everybody think at you is like having a weird radio station that plays all sorts of odd and out-of-tune stuff. It was terrible. And finally, I had someone who understood. But when I found out what she'd done, it made it that much worse. The one person I could finally really, truly trust turned out to be crazy."

Orson whined in sympathy. *I feel you. The only ones who get me are nuts too.*

Sheila laughed and swatted at his ears. "But because we were so linked when I was young, I can always hear her. I can always feel her when she's in trouble. And I can only ignore it for so long."

I held her close to me. "I know. Grown-ups suck. I learned that a long time ago."

She sighed, and some of the tension left her body. "Yeah. They really do."

"I guess that's why I have the mind of a thirteen-year-old."

"And the libido."

I gave her a wink that I was sure was devastatingly sexy. "Positive side effect. Here, let me show you."

And I did... after we put Orson in the bathroom.

SEVEN

The gray-haired mechanic peered at the underside of my Galaxie on the lift. "Yep, it's an axle all right."

Great. "How long will it take?"

He rubbed his hands on his filthy coveralls. "I don't have a part in stock. I can put a call in to Houlton, but they're a small shop too. They probably don't have it, either. The nearest is probably going to be Bangor."

"How long till they can send it up?"

"If they can ship it today, I'll get it tomorrow. And if I get it early enough, I can replace it pretty quick. So, best case is tomorrow around five."

"Worst case?"

"Day after." He looked at a pinup calendar on the wall, the model coyly covering up behind a Goodyear tire. "So Friday."

That wasn't too bad. I could handle another two days in Caribou. "How much?"

"With shipping, parts, and labor, you're looking at about four hundred dollars."

Goddamn moose was sure taking a bite out of my army pension. "Sure, okay." Through the garage bay window, I saw the morning sun glinting off several beat-up cars with For Sale signs in the lot. "Any chance I could use one of those as a loaner while the part comes in?"

"Sure, you can use the red Neon. It runs okay. Heater works. Twenty bucks a day."

I drove out of the garage in the "red" Neon. Really it was more of a rust color, and much of that was natural.

Sheila was with Orson back at the motel, so I decided to take a tour of the thriving metropolis that was the Most Northeastern City in the United States. Ten minutes later, I pulled up to a diner. So, counting the one near the motel, there were two diners in town. Point for Caribou. I liked diners. There was nothing like a hot turkey sandwich on a cold day.

I got a seat inside at a booth with a red vinyl seat and a Formica table. I ordered a cup of coffee and examined the laminated menu. Turkey club. Hot turkey sandwich. Home fries. Yep, it was a diner.

The waitress looked worn down, with frizzy stray hairs escaping the ponytail she'd tied them back into. Must have been a busy breakfast rush.

When she brought the coffee and little packets of cream, she smiled wanly. "You know what you want, hon?"

"A hot turkey sandwich would be great, with mashed potatoes, gravy, and cranberry sauce."

She nodded and walked back to the counter.

I sipped my coffee while I was alone with my thoughts. Well, hoped I was alone with my thoughts. The last couple of days had proved that I couldn't really be sure of that. I loved Sheila, and we said we wouldn't have secrets from each other. Everyone said that, but we all knew it wasn't true. We all have things we don't want to talk about.

I, however, was dating a woman who really could read my mind. I couldn't have secrets from her, and that only went one way. I was used to it. Kind of. Our relationship was a constant reveal of secrets. *I'm a witch. I can talk to my dog. My aunt nearly irradiated Pennsylvania.*

But I'd known what I was getting into when I signed up for it. I had no regrets. Still, it was nice to enjoy a quiet lunch by myself.

"Isn't it? Simple pleasures are the best." A middle-aged man with long, dark hair slid into the bench opposite me. "Hello, Gabriel. I'm Caleb. It's nice to meet you."

I was too shocked to say anything. Caleb took the opportunity to brush the hair out of his eyes and wave to the waitress. She nodded and brought over a cup of coffee. No creamers. She knew his order.

"Thanks, Helen."

"No problem. You want the usual today?"

"Just coffee for now. How's Jimmy doing? Is his cold better?"

Helen smiled and nodded. "Uh-huh. That tea you made him did the trick. Cleared his nose up right away."

"I'm so glad!" Caleb fished a dollar out of his jeans, but Helen waved him off.

"No, no. You wouldn't take any money for the tea. The least you can let me do is give you coffee on the house." She noticed I was still sitting there and topped up my cup. "Are you a patient? Let me tell you, you are in good hands. He gave me a cream for my back last year. I haven't felt that good on my feet since high school. Is it your back acting up?"

No, it's more that he sicced a moose on me last night. That would have been a great conversation starter. Instead, I rubbed the back of my neck and played along. "Yeah, something like that."

"Sorry, don't mean to pry. Your turkey will be out in a minute." She went off to refill other cups on her way back to the counter.

I turned back to Caleb.

He quietly sipped his coffee, never taking his eyes off me. His gaze was warm and inviting. Not cold at all. "I can tell you have questions."

"You probably don't need me to *tell* you that."

He chuckled. "I think that some reports have been greatly exaggerated. My name is Caleb Sharpe. I am a naturopath. I am certified by the AANP. I live in Portland and have an office there, but I do visitations to communities that aren't populous enough to support someone locally.

I come through Caribou a couple days each month. You can look me up on Google."

"So on those couple of days a month you're here, do you dress up in a loincloth and antlers and slash tractor tires?"

He laughed. "Oh, I see you've been to old Mona's. She's a hoot, isn't she?"

"She doesn't think much of you."

"I don't understand why. I bailed her out of jail after that town hearing."

So that much, everyone could agree on. "I heard it was a little contentious."

"A little? She grabbed the mic and started in on the town council and how they had forsaken their sacred obligation to our children, how they had betrayed their life-giving mother for pieces of silver. I thought that was a very nice bit of color, calling them Judases because they wanted to get jobs in town."

"Mona didn't think you disagreed with her."

"I don't, really. I'm just a little more understanding than she is." He waved his arm to point out the few other customers. "How can you tell a town, when all their kids move away to look for work, that they shouldn't build a factory because some trees will get cut down? Believe me, I would love to keep the area unspoiled. There are plants and herbs up here that are hard to find anywhere else. But, the best anyone could have hoped for would be to make sure they complied with EPA guidelines and environmental assessments."

I took a sip of coffee. It had gone cold despite Caleb's warm words. "You seem entirely reasonable."

"Sure. I'm a healer. I understand that there are many reasons why people suffer that have nothing to do with physical ailments. People really can worry themselves sick over things, especially bills and broken homes."

"People worry about threatening letters too."

Caleb frowned. "I didn't send Mona any threatening letters."

"And Mona doesn't care much for harassment, either."

He gave a little shrug. "Who does?"

Caleb's sweetness-and-light act wasn't working on me. I'd only known Mona for a day, but I didn't think she would fake everything she'd told us just to get Sheila up here. It was time to make him drop the façade. "Probably the same people who like to prance around in loincloths and antlers."

Caleb's frowned deeply, and he grabbed my wrist. His hand felt hot—so hot, I thought it might burn me.

You tell that bat she had better not cause me any difficulties, or I will make trouble for her.

I shook my wrist free. Caleb's eyes had darkened. The kindly-healer face was slipping.

He went on, speaking aloud this time. He tried to smile again, but the effect wasn't the same. "You'd do well to ignore anything that crazy hippie tries to tell you. She's a nut. Mostly harmless but still a loon. You should just walk away from here and never look back."

"That's not an option right now. By the way, you owe me four hundred dollars. For my car."

He snorted. "I can't take any responsibility for your driving. Besides, everyone around here knows to watch out for deer... and moose."

The bell on the door jangled.

Caleb nodded hello to a policeman who had just come in. "Isn't that right, Officer Jones?"

"Oh, hi, Caleb! What's right?"

"That you have to keep an eye out for moose around here."

"You bet! We get at least a couple accidents with them every winter. Heard tell of one last night. Moose just wander into the road and then get hit."

"How's your stomach feeling, Mike?"

"Fantastic!" The cop patted his ample belly. "Those herbs you gave me really help with the digestion."

They shook hands, and the cop went over to a booth.

Caleb turned back to me. He smiled and took ten dollars out of his pocket. "Consider lunch a gift from me. But tell Mona to knock it off. I really haven't gotten angry. Yet."

He left the diner just as Helen came over with my food. I had lost my appetite.

"I'm really sorry, but I can't eat that right now. Can you box it up for me?"

"Oh, did Caleb tell you not to? Part of the treatment?"

"Something like that. Can you bring me a check?"

She fished it out of her apron pocket and placed it on the table. Caleb's ten was more than enough to cover it. I got my order to go and got out.

EIGHT

When I got back to the motel room, Sheila was waiting at the door, wringing her hands. She flung herself at me and hugged me. "Where did you go?"

"What do you mean? I went to the mechanic."

"I know, but... I couldn't tell where you were."

"What?"

"I couldn't *feel* you."

I disentangled myself. "I'd bet that had something to do with my lunch companion."

I told her about Caleb, and she reacted as well as I'd thought she would.

"The nerve of that man!" She balled her fists as if she were going to go find him and punch him. "Trying to threaten you! All but admitting he sent the moose after us!"

"He didn't admit to anything. Just told me to drive better. And it looks like he's much more popular with the locals than Mona. The waitress was swooning over him, and he was all buddy-buddy with the cop. I hate to say it, but no one will ever believe Mona over him. He seems to have charmed everyone."

Sheila laughed and rolled her eyes to the ceiling. "I do believe him when he says Mona called everyone in town an environmental Judas. That's just like her."

"Sounds like her. He claims that he hasn't sent her any letters or harassed her or even spoken to her since he bailed her out. That I don't believe."

I felt warm breath on my feet. I looked down and saw Orson trying to look all cute and innocent.

Something smells good.

I sat down at the small table by the window and unpacked the food while Orson sat expectantly. "You want some turkey? I didn't feel like sitting around the diner after he left."

Orson chuffed at me like I was dumb for asking. The waitress had been nice enough to give me paper plates, so I plopped a chunk of turkey on one and set it down for him.

I started to ask Sheila if she wanted some, but her expression told me she had other things on her mind. "He blocked me out."

"You said."

"I tried to feel you, you know, to make sure you were okay. I was nervous."

I shrugged. "It's okay. Nothing happened. He just wanted to try and intimidate us a bit. Try and send us running."

She still looked concerned. "Why didn't you come back right away?"

"I did. I came here right after he left."

"No, why not come back from the mechanic right away?"

"What?"

"You could have come and gotten us."

"I was just hungry." Anger start to burn inside me, a faint ember I hadn't felt in a long time. "Why do I have to account for my every second? And why were you spying on me?"

"I wasn't!"

"You said that you couldn't sense me. Which means you were either trying to sense me or had been keeping track of me and then lost me."

"I was just worried. We were attacked last night!"

"And I just wanted a few minutes to myself."

"Well, I'm sorry, but you don't have that option right now."

I bristled. My spine stiffened, and I crossed my arms. It was petty, but it pushed on one of my buttons. I had spent my life as part of a larger unit. Family, school, army, and now lovers. But I had always been able to keep a part of myself.

"Really? Do I have to ask to go to the bathroom now?"

I always have to. Don't see why you get special treatment.

Thanks, Orson. Always helpful.

Sheila glared at me. "I'm sorry. That came out wrong. I always—always—keep tabs on you and Orson. It's just second nature for me. You are the two most important beings in my life, and between my crazy aunt and that Caleb person, I need to keep you both close to me. I can't do this without your strength. I can barely keep it together around her." She sank on the foot of the bed and held her head in her hands.

You made her cry!

Yeah, good for Mr. Macho Man. I sighed and tried to put an arm around her, but Orson rewarded me with a growl.

You don't make Mama cry.

Orson hadn't growled at me in a long time, either. Sorry, buddy. I said to Sheila, "I'm sorry."

She took my hand. "It's okay." Then she patted Orson. "It's okay. Don't worry."

But I did worry. I wanted to get the hell out of this place as soon as I could. "So, should we warn the police?"

Sheila sighed. "I guess we have to. But I know no one is going to believe us."

"Maybe we should talk to Mona again."

"Going back there is less appealing to me."

No more moose.

I scratched Orson. "I'm with you. I don't think the beater the me-chanic lent me would make it through a collision with a hedge. Maybe we can meet her somewhere else?"

"Where?"

"Why don't you call her and..."

Sheila closed her eyes and rubbed her temple. A few seconds later, she looked up. "There's a place in Presque Isle that she likes. No one's banned her from there. Yet."

"What... I'm not going to get used to that."

"Come on, we'll meet her there."

Wait! Orson was practically bouncing in place as he whined. *We can't go yet!*

Sheila bent down to him. "Why? What's wrong?"

I didn't finish my turkey.

NINE

We found Twin Peaks Coffee near the college campus. It was a quiet little storefront. Only its tinted windows differentiated it from the neighboring buildings. It was full of comfy overstuffed armchairs, small tables, and funky paintings, no doubt from local artists. It was empty except for Mona, who was sitting at a table and sipping a cup of tea. The only other person in the place was the barista, a college-aged girl with multicolored hair, who was behind the display case counter.

Mona spotted us and waved us to her table. "Come! Sit down. Becky, bring them some coffee!"

"You got it, Mona!" She emerged from behind the counter, carrying a tray with two cups of coffee, sugar packets, and a small pitcher of cream. Becky had a nipple ring. I saw this because Becky was topless. "Anything else I can get you? We've got some great cinnamon buns."

I bit my tongue hard enough to draw blood. I still got a kick in the shin from Sheila.

"Uh, no," I stuttered. "We're good for now."

"Well, if you change your mind, just give a holler." She winked and walked back to the counter.

Sheila finally found her voice. "What the hell?"

Mona smirked and waved her hand dismissively. "Oh, Sheila, don't be a prude!"

"What kind of place is this?"

"It's a coffee shop, of course."

"Of course? You didn't tell me about the... the..." Sheila gestured across her chest.

Mona shrugged. "I told you it was called Twin Peaks! What did you expect?"

"It's a college town. I thought they were David Lynch fans."

Mona stared blankly. "Who?"

"You know, the TV show."

"Oh, sweetie, I haven't owned a TV since they canceled *Dynasty*."

Orson sat next to us. *Why does she have an earring there?*

I shrugged and took a sip from my cup. "The coffee's good, at least."

Sheila glared at me disapprovingly. "You're going to drink that? I'm not convinced their health code standards are up to par."

Mona laughed. "Oh, you sound just like the town council! They said the same thing. But they couldn't prove anything. Otherwise, they'd have shut them down." Mona drank some coffee and continued. "Anyway, it's such an empowering place! I know the owner—she's a great old broad. It's not some sleazy strip bar. It's all very body positive, with women of all ages and sizes behind the counter. I even worked a few shifts in support when the council was threatening them."

I tried not to choke.

Mona pressed on. "So tell me what happened."

I told her about my lunch date with Caleb.

Mona was indignant and threw her hands up. "You saw the letters! *Someone* is sending them to me!"

"We believe you," Sheila said. "I know you aren't lying. About that."

"What do you mean?"

"I don't think you were as polite as you said you were at the town meeting."

Mona frowned. "Maybe I wasn't. But so what? The people here were being shortsighted! They were sacrificing their future for what? A little money?"

Sheila sighed. "We're on your side. We are trying to help, but you aren't making it easy."

"I'm sorry. I know you're helping. It's just that no one else believes me."

"Yeah," I said. "Caleb's trying to make us think you're crazy, but moose don't act like that. They wander into the road and get hit by cars—they don't charge you." That was what the cop at the diner had said.

Mona looked worried. "Did you warn the police?"

"No," I said. "They all seem to like Caleb. I can leave a tip that someone is going to blow it up, but I don't know what it's going to do."

"And you're sure he's going to do something?" Sheila asked.

"Yes! I'm positive! I know it. I can *feel* it. You, of all people, should know what that's like."

Sheila's eyes narrowed. She was about to let loose on Mona when the server interrupted her.

"Can I get you anything else?"

Sheila turned her head quickly—then, remembering the shop's uniform, she closed her eyes and thumped the table with her fist. "No, thanks. We're heading out soon." *And if you look at her, Gabe, I will hurt you.*

The server left, and Sheila started in on Mona again. "You're family. I'm here. I am helping you. But don't act like we're peas in a pod. Now, let's try and figure out how we can—"

Bam!

We turned our heads. A pigeon had crashed into the window, leaving a smear on the glass.

"Does that happen a lot?" I asked, gaping at the stunned bird lying on the sidewalk.

"No, never," Becky answered. "We tinted the windows to keep out the lookie-loos. It also keeps birds from hitting it."

Bam! Another pigeon.

Sheila shook her head. "It doesn't seem to be working."

Bam! Bam! Two seagulls joined the pile.

"What the hell?" I said. "Why on earth are—"

Then the deluge hit. *Bam! Bam! Bam! Bam!* Dozens of birds—thrushes, chickadees, and woodpeckers—slammed into the window. Cracks started to appear. Then an owl dove in. *Bam! Crash!* The window shattered. Cold air and birds whirled into the room. We dove under the table. Becky screamed and ran into the kitchen. The air was thick with feathers. Orson barked and snapped at any birds that flew too close.

Sheila and Mona ducked for cover then locked eyes. Holding hands, they closed their eyes. I felt rather than heard a hum from them. A pulse radiated out from the two women, knocking me on my ass. I was dizzy, and the birds were too. They dropped out of the air and landed with a resounding chorus of thumps.

I shook my head clear and sat up. I was a few feet away from where I had been sitting. All the tables and chairs were pushed back to the edges of the room. Birds littered the floor except for an empty circle around Mona and Sheila. Most of them were staggering around and trying to fly off.

"We need to go." Sheila grabbed me and Orson and dragged us out of the café with Mona close behind.

TEN

Mona jumped into her jeep and drove off. We piled into our loaner car, and I sped off as well. The Neon was covered with bird shit but was otherwise unharmed.

"What the hell was that?"

Sheila sighed. "I'm guessing it was proof that Mona wasn't joking about Caleb. Unless you think being attacked by Maine wildlife twice in two days was a coincidence."

"I meant the power surge."

"Oh. Just something we used to do when I was a kid. We would be outside and getting eaten by mosquitos. It was a trick Mona did to stun them and turn them away. We just amped it up a little for the birds."

Like riding a bike, I guessed. There are some things a person doesn't forget.

Sheila went on. "How did Caleb know we were here?"

I shrugged. "Maybe he followed Mona."

Maybe he followed you.

I glanced back at Orson in the rearview mirror. A few feathers still clung to his coat. He looked very annoyed.

Bet you didn't check.

He was right. I was mad at Caleb and hadn't been thinking. It would have been easy for him to follow me back to the motel. He probably thought we would check back in with Mona to see how much of what he'd said was true. That meant he knew where we were staying, which was not a comforting thought.

"Shit."

Yeah.

Sheila looked at me. "Do you think he knows where we are?"

"Even if he didn't follow me, it's not like it would be hard to find us. There aren't a lot of motels in town, and they darn sure aren't busy in January."

Sheila sounded worried. "Do you think he'll do anything?"

WE GOT OUR ANSWER TO Sheila's question when we pulled up to the motel. A police cruiser and an animal control van were parked haphazardly in the lot, and the driveway was blocked with caution tape. I recognized the cop from the diner standing at the parking lot entrance.

He waved us away as I pulled up. "Sorry, folks, you can't come in."

"What's going on?" I asked. "We're staying here."

The cop shook his head. "You'll have to wait. A black bear wandered into the lot and got into one of the rooms."

All I needed was one guess as to which. I spotted a broken window about halfway down. I put the car in park and got out to get a better look. Orson jumped onto Sheila's lap and poked his head out the window.

A small crowd had formed to watch the show. Through the broken room window, I saw a decent-sized black bear chowing down on the contents of a take-out box.

Hey, he's eating my turkey!

"Not yours anymore, Orson."

The guy in an animal control uniform held a tranquilizer gun, but he apparently didn't want to drag the beast out of the room. Instead of using the gun, he was trying to lure it outside with a little pile of fruit and a cheeseburger just outside the room.

"Think that'll work?"

I would follow him anywhere.

"Glad to know where your loyalties lie."

A murmur rippled through the crowd around me. An older guy in a battered Red Sox cap spoke to his buddy. "So weird to see a bear out now."

His friend wearing an orange hunting vest replied, "Yeah, they should be hibernating. Musta woke up early."

Sox Cap scratched his stubble. "Yeah, must be starvin'. No wonder he came inta town."

Hunting Vest rubbed his neck. "Poor sap just had some takeout in there. Bear musta smelled it."

"Yeah, teach that come-from-away to keep food in his room."

They both chuckled and watched as the bear lumbered out of the doorway. It had finished the turkey and was still hungry. As soon as the bear gulped down the cheeseburger, animal control shot the dart into it. The bear chuffed and growled then lurched forward a few feet before slumping over. The crowd cheered and started to break up. The show was over.

Eventually, the bear was loaded into a van and driven off to woodsier pastures. The police took down the caution tape, and we were able to check out the damage.

The room was trashed. The motel owner told us the bear had gotten in through the door when the maid came in to clean. She was so terrified, she'd smashed the front window with a chair and dove through. The beds were wrecked, and there was snow and mud everywhere. And there was so much bear crap.

Most of our stuff was all right. My bag was on top of the dresser, and Sheila's was in the closet. The bear had seemingly ignored them to get to the turkey.

The owner apologized profusely and offered us a free room for the rest of our stay. Sheila wasn't interested. "If he knows we're here, he'll just come back and screw with us again," she told me, and I couldn't argue with that.

"Where should we stay?" I asked. "We can't leave until the car's ready, and that's at least tomorrow. We'll be easy to find at any other motel we stay at."

Sheila frowned. "Were you listening in? Yes, I know, but..." Then she looked at me, resigned to her fate. "There is one place."

"You mean..."

"Yeah. Mona's getting the sleeping bags out."

Scones!

We both glared at Orson. "Shut up," we said in unison.

ELEVEN

I tried my best to put a good spin on things. "Well, at least we can watch each other's backs out here. We'll be protected."

Sheila just glared at me.

I stopped trying to make it better and went back to concentrating on inching our way through the ruts and craters of Mona's drive. It was midafternoon and already getting dark.

Scones!

Orson, at least, would be happy.

We made it through the ruts and potholes and stopped in front of Mona's house.

She was at the door to greet us, less cheerful than yesterday. "The fire's going, and I made up the guest room."

Sheila nodded. "Thanks."

"And I've got a pot of soup on the stove. It should be ready soon."

Sheila nodded again, but no one moved.

Orson nudged things along by trotting into the open door. *Come on, it's cold out here!*

No argument from me. I followed Orson, then Sheila and Mona came in after me. The woodstove was blazing, and it was delightful. But that was the only warm thing in the cottage. The chill Sheila was giving off could have flash-frozen vegetables. And Mona wasn't a lot better, offers of soup notwithstanding.

Once we were seated with cups of hot tea, Mona finally broke the silence. "*Now* do you believe me? Or do you think I sent moose and birds and bears after you?"

Moose and birds and bears, oh my!

I couldn't help but grin at Orson.

Sheila grimaced. "Of course I believed you. I always believe, and I always come when you need me. You just... leave things out sometimes."

"Like what?"

Sheila glared at her, and even I could read her thoughts. *Don't even.*

Mona glared back. "No, really, what have I left out? I've been honest about everything!"

"Really? You were just peacefully explaining yourself at that meeting, huh?"

"Oh, come on! I may have downplayed that a little, but only because I know how you get. So judgmental."

Sheila's eyes flared with rage. "And why do you think that might be?"

"I have no idea."

"Really? None whatsoever? Not even nearly blowing up the Eastern Seaboard? You think that should escape judgment?"

"You weren't even alive back then. You have no idea what it was like. One militaristic, rampaging, imperialist country trying to wipe their mirror image off the map."

"That didn't give you any right to do—"

"To do what? I didn't cause a meltdown. I didn't build the plant with terrible safety controls. You know how these things get built, right? Lowest-bid contracts! Cut every corner to save taxpayer money, and then the contractors cut every corner to increase *their* profit margin. You'll be lucky if the damn building doesn't blow over in a stiff breeze!"

Mona was right about that. That was how I'd wound up in a Humvee without armor in Iraq.

Sheila shot me a look. *Stay out of this!*

Mona jumped in. "Don't get mad at him! He's not the problem! The problem is that you never believed in what I was doing."

Sheila raised her voice to match Mona's. "How could I? You could have killed thousands of people!"

Mona was practically shouting now. "Compared to what? The millions I saved?"

"Hypothetically saved. Versus those—"

"I didn't kill anyone. Hypothetically or otherwise. No one died because of me." Sheila started to say something, but Mona cut her off. "No. I do not apologize for anything I did. Now or then. I cannot stand by while people destroy our home and provider. Our power comes from the earth, and it is up to us to do everything we can to protect it. *Everything.* You'd do well to remember that."

"I know!"

"Do you? That's why I'm up here. Goodness knows I can do without the snow. But Mother Earth is strong here. Strong and powerful because it hasn't been disturbed. There is strength and beauty here, but it will only last if we stand up for it."

Sheila's voice got quiet, the way she got when she was doing her best to contain all her rage. "We aren't supposed to kill. You taught me that long ago."

"There's murder, and then there's self-defense."

Sheila got angrier. "Was that nuclear meltdown 'self-defense'?"

Mona was unfazed. "Of course. If we let them rape and destroy that which we hold most sacred, we may as well join in. You don't get points for good intentions. Only results."

All was silent. Then Sheila slumped in her seat. "I can't make you see reason. I can't change your mind. Tomorrow, we will tell the police about the threats, but then we're done. I can't do this anymore."

Sheila rose and went into the bedroom. Orson followed. I took a last sip of tea and went after them. Mona was concentrating on her tea as I closed the door.

TWELVE

"That self-righteous zealot... bitch!"

I was shocked. Orson covered his ears with his paws and whined.

Sheila kept shouting as she stormed around the small room. "Do you get it now? Do you understand why I can't stay here anymore? She can always push my buttons."

"You know, a very wise and beautiful woman once told me that people can only push your buttons if you let them."

She spun on her heel and pointed a finger at me. "*Do not* quote me right now."

"Just trying to help."

"Well, help by getting the car fixed faster to get us out of here."

She knew I couldn't do anything about the car, but I thought it best not to remind her of that. "Come on, we're here for a night. Like you said, we'll leave early tomorrow and go to the police, get the car, and head somewhere warmer."

"And far away." She flopped down on the bed.

"Sure," I said. "Miami's nice."

"Hawaii?"

"Don't think the convertible would like that."

She smiled a bit but shook her head. "It doesn't matter. Some things you can't escape from. We could drive to the moon, and she'd still find a way to be a burden on me." She leaned over, elbows on her knees, and rubbed her temples and forehead. She only did that when she felt a headache coming on.

I tried to change tack. "So, what Mona said about the earth being the source of your power, is that right?"

Sheila didn't even look up. "Of course. Where else would it come from?"

"Well, I don't know. It is magic, right?"

"Sure, but that's where it comes from. The energy of this world has existed since long before we humans have. It is precious and powerful, and we have to protect it." Sheila sighed. "And that's why I can't help but let her under my skin. In so many ways, she's absolutely right."

"What?"

"I'm not about to blow anyone up. But that part of her that wants to defend and protect us and make sure our Mother is safe—that, I can't argue with. And she's right that the energy is stronger here. Much stronger than I'm used to."

"What do you mean?"

"I usually have to keep myself wide-open to feel the energy. It's hard to receive it among the people and crowds and buildings of a big city. And believe me, that's a balancing act. Trying to block out the crowd noise while opening yourself up, it's like playing Name That Tune with earplugs in. But here, it's just everywhere. It's why I've been on edge lately. Every nerve is tingling with it. I don't know if it's because we're in unspoiled land, like Mona said, or if there's another reason for it, but it is overwhelming."

That was something. I had learned a lot, but I still didn't know that much about witches. I did know that Sheila was incredibly strong. If it was a lot for her to handle, then Mona must be at least as strong to cope with it full-time. No wonder she seemed a little batty.

After Sheila massaged out her headache, we lay down to sleep. Sheila's soft breathing meant she had drifted off quickly, as did Orson's gentle chuffing. I heard some banging in the kitchen, which I guessed was Mona putting away the teacups. Then everything was quiet. All were asleep, and I soon was as well.

I AWOKE WITH A START. I felt like something was wrong, but it was nothing more than a vague feeling. I had no idea what time it was. The room was pitch-black and completely quiet. I had never understood the phrase "deafening silence" until then. The stillness was so absolute that all I could hear was the blood thrumming in my ears. Not even Orson's or Sheila's breathing. It was oppressive. I could feel it all around me.

I tried to focus and clear my head, but it still felt full of cobwebs. I rolled over to Sheila and was about to shake her to wake up when she sat up, eyes open and fully alert.

"I know. I feel it too."

"What is it?"

She shook her head. "I don't know. I just can feel something out there."

There was a knock at the door. Before it had finished, Sheila called out, "Yes, Mona. We know. We're up."

"Glad to hear it. This feels bad."

"We're coming. Come on, Orson."

Orson didn't respond.

"Orson? Orson!"

Mmmm...

Sheila got a little agitated. "Wake up."

Mmmm...

He moved slowly. He wasn't asleep but seemed groggy. I guessed the cold weather wasn't agreeing with him.

Sheila was dressing quickly, so I tried to talk to him. "You okay, pal?"

Orson just growled. He'd never really been a morning dog. I shrugged and pulled on my jeans and a sweatshirt. Sheila ran out of the bedroom, and I followed. She joined Mona at the front window, looking out into the darkness.

"What time is it? What's going on?"

Mona answered me. "About three a.m. And I'm not sure."

Sheila looked at me. "I can't tell what's out there, either. Just that it's nothing we want a part of."

I peered through the window into the blackness. I couldn't see anything, either. Big help I was. All I could tell was that it was cold. Wisps of frost curled across the corners of the window.

"So, why are we all up?" I asked.

Mona and Sheila looked at each other and nodded.

"Something's out there," Sheila answered.

"Something?"

"Or someone," Sheila continued. "I can't quite tell."

"You can't..." I gestured at my head.

"No. I can't tell. I'm being blocked."

Mona answered the question forming in my head. "It's him. It has to be."

Caleb. Had this been the plan? Get us all together and deal with us all at once? Or were we just in the wrong place? That was happening a lot, and I didn't care for it.

I cared for it a lot less when I heard—or more precisely, *felt*—the voice, inside my head.

Hello, Mona. It was him.

Sheila looked at me, and I nodded to let her know I'd heard it too.

"Broadcasting on all frequencies," I said.

We told you. We warned you to stay out of the way.

Go fuck yourselves. Mona did not like to get pushed around.

I heard the throaty chuckle in my head. *Oh, Mona, we could have worked so well together. Why do you fight us? We want the same thing.*

You don't know me.

Oh, I know you all too well. The Mona I've known about would help us destroy that abomination of a factory.

I could see them as they appeared out of the darkness, one at a time. They wore the same loincloths Mona had shown us. They were so bright against the black woods, they seemed to glow. Finally, one figure wearing antlers stepped forward. Caleb. He was staring right at us.

It would be best for you to join us. Tomorrow, that mill will be destroyed, but tonight, we start with you.

He raised his arms to the sky and started to chant. The others joined him. Then I felt a rumble. I remembered what Mona had shown us at the groundbreaking, where the loincloth crew had caused an earthquake. There, they had made frozen ground crack open. Mona's cottage was ramshackle at best; it wouldn't last long.

Not today.

Mona looked at Sheila. Sheila nodded. They clasped hands and closed their eyes. I felt the rumbling grow fainter. I smiled. Caleb may have had a few tricks, but they couldn't compete with my lady and her dog.

Wait... Where is he?

Orson was groggy getting up, but there was no way he would ignore Sheila if she needed him. I looked out and saw Caleb gesture to his followers. They seemed to double down on the chanting. Mona's cottage shuddered, and a crack formed in the picture window. Sheila and Mona exchanged worried glances, and Sheila quickly looked for Orson.

I felt a sharp, searing pain in my leg. *What the hell?* I looked down and saw Orson clinging to my calf.

"Orson! Let go!"

He didn't. Sheila turned to look at me, and her jaw dropped. "Orson! Stop that!"

He growled and bit down harder. I yelled in pain. Sheila turned away from the window and lunged at him.

Mona shouted at her. "No! Don't get distracted!"

With a loud crack, the floor split open about a foot wide. Mona fell backward as Sheila tried to pry Orson off me.

"Orson! Orson, no!" Sheila grabbed him, both arms around his neck, and tried to coax him off me. After a second, the familiar golden flecks sparked in his eyes, and he loosened his grip on me. I freed my leg and hopped back from them, but Orson still growled at me.

Mona screamed behind us. The crack in the floor had widened. It had reached the walls, and the roof was about to come down on us.

I tried to run to Sheila. She saw me coming and shook her head. She flung her arm out at me, and I felt myself flying backward out the window and into the night. Then all went black.

THIRTEEN

Cold... so cold. I opened my eyes. I was in the woods, lying on my side, my cheek buried in a snowdrift. I tried to pick myself up off the ground. Mona, Sheila, and Orson were nowhere to be seen.

Orson...

What the hell? What had happened? Orson had never done that before. Even when he was mad at me, even when Sheila and I argued, he'd never *bitten* me.

I thought about the creatures that had plagued us. Even with Caleb's ability to control animals, Orson's bond with Sheila was surely stronger than that...

Wasn't it?

I brushed off the snow and looked around. I didn't see anyone else. Sheila... The house had been coming down as she'd flung me clear. Oh no.

I guessed at what direction Mona's house was and tried to run. I took one step and almost fell over in pain. The bite Orson had left on my leg was throbbing. I hopped over to the trunk of a sturdy tree and leaned against it. Blood oozed out of the bite mark. He'd really tried to tear a chunk out of my leg.

Four days ago, we had watched the sunset on the Gulf of Mexico. We'd sat on a beach, Sheila leaning on me, our fingers intertwined, while Orson had bounded in the surf happily.

Fuck Maine. Fuck Caleb. Fuck this.

All right. Enough self-pity. Regroup. Replan.

I looked around the trees and found a stick I could lean on. It was short, so I ended up hunched over and limping. Better than hopping or crawling in the snow.

I shivered. I guessed it was single digits out, and my sweatshirt wasn't going to cut it for long. I limped into the clearing.

Oh no.

The house was a ruin. The crack in the foundation had caused the walls to buckle and the roof to come down. I tried to run closer, but it was more like hopping and lurching.

"Sheila! Orson!" I screamed.

I didn't hear—or feel—anything. It was silent. All I could hear was my own breathing. I tried to calm down while watching my hot breath crystallize into mist.

Then I heard a soft moan coming from near the edge of the clearing, then a cough.

"Sheila!" I lurched closer. I couldn't feel her. If she were awake, she would have been in my head already. I saw something move. It looked like a blanket or a pile of rags coming to life.

With a sigh, the pile rolled over. It was Mona. She coughed and looked up at me. "Mother Goddess! That one can pack a wallop!"

"Caleb?"

Mona started to laugh, but it turned into a coughing fit. "Guess again, sweetie."

I looked at the field. The trees on the edge had been pushed outward. Rather than collapsing inward, the walls of the house had been sent forward. "Sheila?"

Mona grinned then wheezed. "She always was a firecracker."

I sat down in the snow. The pain in my leg and the display of Sheila's protective anger was too much. "Sheila did this?"

"Yep. She pushed you away to get you safe and took half my cottage along with it."

I shouldn't have been surprised. Sheila was protective of us, and when we were threatened, she got angry. There was a wannabe witch in a supermax cell who could tell a great story about how Sheila had tried to drop a theme park on her because she'd made Sheila think she had hurt me.

"Where is Sheila?" I asked.

"I don't know. Last thing I saw was my house falling down around me."

I looked around frantically. "What happened to Caleb and the Lost Boys?"

She shrugged. "As soon as the house came down, they went back into the woods."

I was still a bit groggy. "I remember Orson biting me. Then I remember the roof cracking. Then I remember falling away and waking up in the snow."

"Right."

"I thought you and Sheila were doing something to counter Caleb, and when Orson distracted her, that spell was broken."

"That's right."

"But that didn't wreck your house?"

"No, he's not strong enough to stop both me and Sheila. She's a natural."

But he was strong enough to turn Orson against us...

"Sheila got distracted. He was able to use that to crack the roof. Sheila panicked and got you clear. Probably her and Orson too."

"Can't you tell? You can find her telepathically, right?"

"Well..."

I was losing patience. "Where are they? Are they under that roof over there or not?"

"I don't know!"

"What do you mean? Find her! You could call her in Florida. Right now, she can't be more than a few hundred yards away!"

Mona looked worried for the first time. "I don't know, because I can't hear her. She could be unconscious. She could be just blocking me."

I shook my head. "I don't think she'd try and block you right now. Get up. We have to find her and figure this out."

We limped back to the shambles that was the house. We found no one else there. Thank God. I did find my coat and some better shoes. Mona found a flashlight. I trudged through the woods nearby and saw several sets of footprints, at least ten. No doubt they were from Caleb's little friends.

Then I found a set of footprints next to a set of small paw prints. They were heading up to the main road. I tried to follow them, but my leg wasn't having any of it. The cold and the broken ground made me retreat back to the house.

"It looks like they ran out of here," I told Mona. "Either they're walking down the road or got in a car." *Or were forced into one.* I didn't say that out loud.

Mona tried to reassure me. "She can take care of herself. She's tough."

"I know." I wished I felt as sure as I'd tried to sound.

I went back to check on our crappy Neon. A brick or stone had bashed the front driver's-side panel, but the dent seemed superficial, and it blended in with the rest. The car started, and I managed to get it back onto the rutted road.

I called to Mona. "Come on, get in."

"Where are you going?"

"We have to find Sheila and get out of here."

"She's tough. She's going to be okay."

I was getting tired of hearing that. "You keep saying that, but you can't hear her."

Mona spread her hands. "If she wasn't in the wreckage, then I'm sure she's all right."

"I have to check. Stay if you want, but I'm going."

I put the car in drive and stepped on the gas. Then I stopped short. There was a monster in front of me.

FOURTEEN

It was tall and rail thin. At least seven feet. Hooves on the bottom, antlers on the top, human in the middle. Gray fur on the legs, taut gray skin on the torso. The head was awful and misshapen, like a caribou head that had been mashed into a man's skull and stitched together. It was bone. No skin or fur covered it, but there was light in the eyes. Sharp bones protruded at odd angles, spiky ribs and elbows, all covered with ropy muscle.

What the fuck...

It reared its head back and shrieked. The bloodcurdling sound was full of pain and anger. Then it stared straight into my eyes.

Smarter men than me would have backed away. However, as many had pointed out to me, I was not a smart man.

Fuck this. I gunned the engine and ran right at it.

That caught it by surprise. I'm sure it hadn't expected some crazy idiot to try to ram it with a tiny toy car. I plowed into it. Then I found out two things. First, the Neon had working airbags. And second, big things did fall hard.

The creature wailed and fell backward, hitting the cold ground with a thud. I tried to back up and run over it, but the engine was having none of that. The hiss of steam told me that the radiator was probably shot. I remembered seeing a tire iron behind the driver's seat when I got in the car that morning. I felt behind me. *Yes.*

I jumped out and went around to the thing in front. It was shaking its horrible skull, but it seemed more startled than hurt. When it started to stand up, I ran in and hit it on the head with the tire iron. I got in two good hits, full on. I heard the thwack of the metal and an echoing ring. That slowed it down for a second. Then it was on its feet.

I reared my arm back, ready to swing again, but I found that hard to do with its hand around my throat. It was fast. I could barely register how cold and clammy the hand felt as it lifted me off the ground.

I tried to hit its arm with the tire iron while using my free hand to pry its fingers off my throat. Neither worked very well. The light in its eyes glowed. I couldn't see the mouth move, but I heard the low guttural laugh.

I dropped the tire iron and used both hands to pry at the bony fingers, which worked no better. I could make out a commotion behind me. Probably Mona. I hoped she could get off a spell or two before I blacked out. I thrashed and kicked, but it looked like the last thing I saw would be the two dead eyes of the monster in front of me.

Then, with a crash, a pine tree slammed into the creature. It fell to the side, dropping me. I drew a few ragged breaths and rolled away. I looked up.

Sheila and Orson burst through the forest edge. Fury seemed to radiate off Sheila, and Orson was snarling and barking next to her. She was screaming, throwing wildly with her arms. Each pitch of her arm uprooted a tree and flung it at the monster. Most were right on target, bashing into it, knocking it farther back each time. That didn't seem to hurt it all that much, but it was enough to keep the creature off-balance.

Finally, it had had enough. The thing shrieked and turned to run into the woods. Sheila started to follow, but Orson saw me and barked. Sheila turned to me, still furious, and seemed torn between helping me and hunting the monster.

"Sheila! Calm down and help us out!" Mona shouted from behind us.

As if seeing me for the first time, Sheila blinked, and the tension in the air dissipated.

"Gabe... Oh no, are you all right?"

I nodded. "I've been through worse. I'll be okay."

She knelt and hugged me close. "Oh goodness, I was so worried. When I saw that thing go after you, I almost lost it."

"What was that? I've never seen... anything like that."

"Caleb."

I didn't understand. "Caleb controls it?"

"No. It is Caleb."

FIFTEEN

I was stunned. "I'm sorry. I met Caleb. He's not seven feet tall with a deer skull for a head. Is it a mask? Is this Scooby-Doo?"

"No. It's him. It's all him."

"I hit it with a car and a tire iron. You threw a forest at it. How can he be doing this?"

Sheila rocked back and sat on the cold ground, clearly exhausted. She looked at the remains of Mona's cottage. "After Orson bit you and the roof cracked, I got a little angry."

I couldn't help but grin. "Really?"

Sheila blushed a little but only a little. "Don't make me feel guilty for caring about you. I may have lashed out too strongly, but I was only trying to get you and Mona clear."

Mona cackled. "Sweetie, I need to break out my old yurt, thanks to you."

"Again, sorry. But I was a little freaked out about my familiar turning against me." She glared at Orson.

Lying on the ground as flat as he could, Orson whined pitifully and covered his eyes with his paws. *I'm sorry.*

"You'd better be," Sheila said. "What happened?"

When you woke me up, everything felt... off. I felt groggy. Didn't feel like myself. Then, I suddenly felt like I had to defend you. From Gabe. Orson crawled over to me and put his head on my leg. He looked up at me with his big, sad eyes. *I'm sorry.*

I scratched his head. "Can't stay mad at you, buddy. Even if I'll never walk again."

Orson whined.

"Kidding! I'm sorry, pal."

Orson licked where he had bitten me and keened softly.

Sheila leaned over and rubbed his back. "Even if Orson was asleep, even if his defenses were down, no one should be able to do that to my dog. It took a lot of focus to get him off you, which took away from defending the house."

Mona chimed in. "That's why he did it. Divide and conquer."

Sheila didn't answer her. "So when the roof cracked and I realized what was happening, I just wanted to get you safe." She looked around the clearing and saw the trees at the far edges pushed outward. "I may have panicked, used too much energy."

Mona bit her tongue.

"It knocked Caleb's people on their asses, and they scattered. But I was focused on Caleb. I chased him into the woods, and that's where it happened."

"What?" I asked.

"It's hard to describe."

"Here, sweetie. Let me help." Mona held out her hand.

Sheila looked at it for a second then nodded. I grabbed a hand from each of them. What I saw was a waking nightmare.

I was running through the woods. I could feel Sheila's anger and the cold air against her hot face. She was livid. I felt a brush against her leg. Orson was running alongside her. I could feel his guilt and confusion. We were chasing Caleb. I could see his antlered mask up ahead, bobbing through the trees. We were gaining on him.

Suddenly, he stopped. He had reached the road by the forest's edge and had ran out of cover. We stopped as well. Caleb was framed in a moonbeam that pierced the clouds. Caleb turned and smiled. His eyes showed through the mask, glowing in the light.

"Very good. I see magic runs in the family, but my family is older and stronger."

He knelt to the ground, touching his hands to the earth, then started to hum and chant under his breath. The ground started to tremble. The chant turned into a scream. I wanted to scream myself. Bones split and lengthened. Muscles moved like snakes under his skin and wove themselves across suddenly broad shoulders. There were cracks and pops as vertebrae snapped into place and a grinding sound as the skull and antlers fused into his head. He reared back and roared. The sound touched something primal in me and made me want to crawl inside my skin and hide. Steam poured out of the nostril slits in the skull as the thing chuffed heavily.

Caleb, or whatever he had become, rose. He was silhouetted in the moonlight, black and powerful, as the antlers spread wide. He pointed at us.

Sheila hesitated for a moment, not believing what she was seeing. Orson leapt ahead, snarling and barking. Caleb was startled for a second. Then he waved his hand as if swatting a fly, and Orson flew back. He banged against a tree and yelped. We ran to him. Caleb took the opportunity to loop around and head back toward the cottage.

I saw Orson. He was dazed and whimpering but okay. Then there was a crash, which I guessed was me ramming the car into Caleb. I ran toward the noise, and Orson and Sheila came with me.

Sheila let go of our hands, and I was staring at her ashen face, stunned.

"How?" I asked.

Sheila shook her head.

Mona was speechless as well. "I've been at this longer than you, but I've never heard of anything like that."

"He mentioned 'Kisulk' before. You told us that was the native creator, right? Their version of God or the big bang."

Mona nodded at me.

"Is he channeling that?"

"I don't know. He's channeling *something*. All the tales of Kisulk that I read were about a benevolent creator. Not destructive."

I spent a lot of time in churches as a kid. I heard a lot about a loving Jesus and a lot more about a wrathful God. "It can't all be sweetness and light."

Mona had no answer. "I never read anything about that, but I'm not an expert."

Sheila shivered. "We need to get out of here."

I looked at the rental car. It wasn't going anywhere, and since Sheila had uprooted a telephone pole, it didn't look like Mona's phone would be working. "Mona, is your car still in one piece?"

We followed her around to the side of the remains of her cottage. Her car was snug by the tree line, out of the line of fire. She had a tiny, boxy four-wheel drive car, a Suzuki Samurai. Aside from a dent in the driver's-side door and one on the roof, it seemed fine. She started the car, and the engine turned over without much complaint. "Let's go. I know a place."

SIXTEEN

We piled into Mona's Samurai. That might have been the most inappropriate name for a car in recorded history. Samurai were noble and skilled warriors. The car, though, was squat and boxy, and it bounced horribly in the ruts on the road. I was sure the owner's manual claimed the car could seat four adults. Mona and Sheila were comfortable up front, while I had my knees up by my chin in the back. Orson had tiny little legs, and he wasn't doing a lot better.

Sheila, exhausted from the night's events, reclined her seat back the few inches it would go and closed her eyes. Then she was out. I was tired as well, but the back seat didn't move. It did go up and down, which happened every time the car hit a pothole. My head was almost touching the roof to start with, and bumping it every few seconds wasn't restful.

I glanced down at Orson. He was curled up, but his eyes were wide-open.

"You okay?"

No.

"You want to tell me about it?"

I'm sorry.

I stroked his head gently. "I know. I told you I'm not mad. I was just surprised."

Thanks.

"Really, though. What happened?"

I don't know! I wish I did.

I rubbed behind his ears. "It's okay, it's okay." He whined, but I could feel his muscles relax. "Just tell me what you remember."

He sniffled. *It's hard. You woke me up, but I didn't feel... awake.*

"It was the middle of the night. I wasn't surprised."

It was like I was in a dream.

"Dogs dream?"

He glared. *Yes. Of very slow cats.*

I smiled. If he could sass me, then he was going to be okay.

I walked through the house, but it didn't feel like I was walking. I saw you and Mama and Mona, and then... I just felt I had to defend Mama.

"Not attack me."

No.

I didn't know if Caleb knew that Orson was Sheila's familiar. If he'd seen us all together, he might have guessed. He probably didn't know that Orson was special for a familiar. Most witches couldn't talk to their animal companions, and most of the ones that could weren't able to use more than a few words. That was probably what saved us. Orson was stronger than Caleb thought.

Still, Caleb was strong enough to affect Orson. And he was smart. He knew something about familiar animals. He knew enough to not try to turn Orson against Sheila, but Caleb was still powerful enough to twist Orson's loyalties. Smart and powerful gave him the winning hand. Ours, however, weren't so good—we weren't as popular as Caleb, and our opponent was clinically insane. That was a losing hand any way we played it.

I couldn't keep my eyes open, but I wasn't going to sleep in Mona's beater box. I sighed and rubbed my eyes. We had to tell the police what we thought Caleb was up to, even though they would never believe us. We couldn't just let the mill get destroyed, though. Dozens of people could get hurt or even killed. Once we warned someone about it, I would be happy to get out of town. I liked a good lobster as much as the next guy, but I could definitely make do with the stone crabs in Florida.

I looked up at Mona. She stared straight ahead with a white-knuckle grip on the wheel. Sheila cried out softly in her sleep. Without shifting her gaze from the road, Mona reached over and stroked her cheek. Sheila murmured and settled down.

We clearly weren't leaving yet.

THE CAR BOUNCED THROUGH a huge rut, jolting me awake. I didn't even realize I'd drifted off. I sat up too quickly and bumped my head on the low ceiling. I grunted and cursed, which woke up Orson.

Come on, man. Let me rest.

"Sorry." I rubbed my head.

Sheila hadn't moved. She was too exhausted and sleeping too soundly to notice my outburst.

Mona turned back to us. "Sorry about that last one. These ruts are a lot worse than the last time I was here." The car bottomed out in another crater. The dream catcher Mona had hung from the rearview mirror swayed and bounced, getting hopelessly tangled up with the black talon strung up next to it. "That wasn't there before."

The pothole was deep enough to swim in. *How long has it been since she was here?*

Mona glared at me. "I'm doing my best. Don't be rude."

I hadn't said anything. The whole mind-reading thing really took some getting used to.

The sun had started to rise. Red light poked through the snow-covered pine trees. We were on a narrow dirt road that was barely more than ruts. If Mona's house was in the middle of nowhere, we'd somehow managed to end up on the other side of nowhere.

"Where are we going?" I asked.

"Somewhere safe."

"Can you be more specific?"

She shook her head. "Not yet. I'm not quite sure where it is."

Great. "Then how do you know…"

Mona cut me off with a grin. "My friend moves around a lot. He doesn't like to stay put for too long. He's a little paranoid." She chuckled. "Not without reason, though."

Orson stretched and yawned. *Gotta pee.*

Mona reached back to scratch Orson. "We'll be there soon. It's not far now."

Orson whined but curled up next to me. In the front, Sheila began to stir. She blinked sleepily then sat up.

Mona rubbed Sheila's knee. "Morning, sleepyhead!"

Sheila groaned. "Where are we?"

"Well, I'm not exactly sure. We're going to check on an old friend. It's safe, at least for a while, and it'll give us time to regroup."

Sheila rubbed her temples. "Does he have coffee?"

Orson chuffed. *Is there bacon?*

After a few more minutes of bouncing, Mona turned off the rutted road into a clearing, where a small camper was attached to a rusty banged-up pickup. A large cross, at least eight feet tall, stood like a ship's mast in the back of the truck, lashed to the cab. Mona rumbled to a stop in front of the camper. A hand-painted wooden sign screwed in above the door read "First Church of God's Creation." It was painted up to look like an unfurled banner.

The door burst open, and a monk bounded out. He was a big guy, with the full beard, tonsured head, and brown robes.

"Mona!" He chortled then wrapped her in a big bear hug.

"Father Rett!" Mona laughed and hugged him back. "I'm so glad we found you."

"No need to be formal. Rett is fine."

"How about 'stud muffin'?" Then Mona kissed him.

It wasn't a little peck on the cheek. As my first girlfriend in seventh grade would have said, it was full-on tonsil hockey. They were at it long enough for the rest of us to get out of the car—and watch uncomfortably. Orson attended to his business at a tree by the camper.

I glanced at Sheila, who shook her head and whispered, "No idea."

Finally, I cleared my throat. After a few seconds, they finally came up for air.

Mona looked back and almost seemed surprised to see us. "Oh! Rett, this is my niece and her fiancé!"

We waved sheepishly. Orson barked. *What about me?*

Rett laughed. "Don't worry, pal! Mona's told me all about you. All of you, in fact."

I didn't find that reassuring.

"Well, come inside!" Rett said. "It's freezing out here, and I have coffee." He led Mona inside.

Sheila and I looked at each other, confused. "Well," she said, "it *is* freezing. And there's coffee." So we followed them into the cramped camper.

A card table occupied the middle of the room. A bookshelf crammed with books and mugs and food items filled one wall. Blankets poked out of the folded-up army cot near the back, where he must have shoved it out of the way when he heard from Mona. More blankets and books were piled up into the mother's attic nook at the front, above a hot plate and an old coffee percolator that hissed and burbled.

An antique space heater was blasting away on the right, making my feet uncomfortably hot. Orson waddled around the left of it, and as soon as he settled down, he curled up and started snoring. Sheila eyed the messy space warily while Mona sat down.

As we inched to our chairs, Rett shuffled around the table and set down the coffeepot and four stained cups. "I don't have a fridge in here, but the cream stays plenty cold up in the cab." He chuckled as he got out a sugar bowl and a carton of half-and-half, then he poured us each a cup of coffee.

Considering how cold and tired I was, it might have been the best cup of coffee ever. It certainly helped after the night we'd just had, and I relaxed a bit. If there had been room, I would have stretched and leaned back. Instead, I just rested my head against the metal wall of the camper.

Rett saw me loosen up after the first sip. "Good, right? These kids at the college did an experiment and grew some coffee hydroponically. The first batch tasted like dirt, but they've gotten a lot better in the roasting process. They make it for a coffee shop in Presque Isle. Twin Peaks, I think. Do you know it?"

I smiled. "Yes, but I didn't pay a lot of attention to the coffee."

"I'll bet." He winked at me.

Sheila rolled her eyes. "No, it was more to do with the swarm of birds that attacked us."

He frowned. "Ah. Yes, Mona told me all about it. I'm sorry that Caleb has been giving you such a hard time."

"Do you know this guy?"

He sighed and took a long sip of his coffee. "Unfortunately, yes. And I'm afraid I owe you an apology."

Sheila and I looked at each other. "Why?"

Rett frowned. "It seems my protégé decided to branch out on his own."

Sheila and I were both shocked, but Sheila found her voice first. "You knew him? You taught him?"

"Yes, but I only taught him about the environment and organizing protests," Rett said, sounding a little defensive. "Anything with the... the..." He waved his hands in an elaborate gesture. "That, I had nothing to do with."

Sheila was not impressed. "You took in that lunatic?"

"Well, he wasn't wearing antlers and a loincloth when I met him. He was just a college kid who didn't think people were taking acid rain and global warming seriously."

I nodded. "I've seen that Caleb. He can be pretty convincing."

Sheila stared at Rett for a minute. I felt a little bad for him. I'd been on the other end of that look a few times. It wasn't easy to brush off. Still, we were the ones who'd been attacked by wildlife, not him.

Rett shifted uncomfortably in his seat. He glanced at Mona, but she was suddenly very interested in her coffee cup. Finally, Rett sighed. "Maybe I should explain."

"Maybe you should." Sheila held his gaze.

SEVENTEEN

"I 've been trying to spread my gospel for over twenty years now," Rett said, gesturing to the bookshelf. I recognized a couple of books, like *Silent Spring* and battered copies of the *Whole Earth Catalog* and *The Anarchist's Cookbook*. The rest of them had similar themes.

"That's what this is?" I asked. "The Church of God's Creation?"

"Yes. I've been going around the country, stopping with allies here and there, trying to wake people up about the crimes against God that are going on in this land." He stared at his cup, eyes blazing with fury.

"Crimes against God?"

"The Bible is full of verses about how we are meant to be stewards of God's creation. Psalm 24 says, 'The Earth is the Lord's, and all it contains.' Genesis 2:15 says, 'God took man and placed him in the Garden of Eden and told him to work it and keep it.' It's very clear that we are meant to take care of this world, and we are doing a piss-poor job of it. Even the Pope's come around to our side!"

"I went to Sunday school as a kid," I said. "I didn't hear a lot about the environment. It was mostly how Satan would get us if we disobeyed our parents."

Father Rett chortled. "I tend to see things a little differently than the official viewpoint. That's probably why I was excommunicated."

Mona cackled. "No kidding!"

Sheila's eyebrows popped up. "They kicked you out?"

"Oh yes." Rett sounded pleased as punch about the whole thing. "They officially branded me a heretic. I got a letter from the archbishop and everything. It was very exciting. They thought I was diluting the message of the church, which at the time, was mainly that gay people were evil and women should be subservient. It was kind of a relief, really. I believe in God, and I believe there is a plan for all of us. I did not believe my plan was for me to lecture people about what they do with their genitals."

He paused for another sip of coffee. "Later, that same archbishop was caught up in the child abuse scandals. He was shuffling pedophile priests from one parish to another. They were fine with forgiveness and keeping *that* bunch in the church. I try and tell people not to pour poison in our drinking water, and I get the boot. They didn't have to sell off half the church properties in Philadelphia to pay for what I did, let me tell you!"

Sheila was skeptical. "Is that really why they kicked you out?"

"I may have been a little overenthusiastic. I really got into it in my sermons. You know those parts about how a camel can more easily pass through the eye of a needle than a rich man can enter heaven? I got into a real fervor about that. How polluters were growing rich by despoiling God's creation. I may have been a little too vocal about the need to deal with those sinners with traditional methods. Like stoning. Or tar and feathers."

"Is Philly where you started out?" I asked.

He pointed to the shelf beside him. "See for yourself." I looked and saw a white hammer in a Lucite case. The hammer had the winged logo of the Flyers on it. I could make out the signature: *#8 Dave 'The Hammer' Schultz.* I smiled. The Hammer was the greatest hockey goon of all time.

Rett pushed up his sleeve to show off his tattoo of a skull-and-crossbones design. The skull was a stylized number eight, and the crossbones were bloody hockey sticks. Orange-and-black blood pooled below it, forming the Flyers insignia. "I got it in '75. I was twenty-two, and the Flyers had just won their second Cup."

I couldn't help needling him a bit. "I thought Jesus asked people to turn the other cheek."

"Yeah, well Jesus never had to play against Bobby Orr and Phil Esposito."

He had a point. "Fair enough."

Rett covered his tattoo. "So, I was a youngster, fresh out of Drexel with my engineering degree. And I managed to find a job with a great new employer in the area. One of the biggest engineering and power projects to come along in a while."

"What was that?" I asked. But before he could answer, the dominos in my mind started to fall into place. *Philadelphia... mid-seventies... power plant...* "Wait... Three Mile Island?"

Rett smiled.

"And I bet Rett is short for something, isn't it?"

He winked at Mona. "You were right—he is a clever one." He turned back to me and Sheila. "Yes, I got a job in the control room in '76. And I was working the night of the accident. And yes, Rett is short for something. My full name is Everett Smith."

Sheila was stunned. "Everett? The same Everett my aunt was dating?"

Rett nodded. "Oh yes. Mona was something back then. She still is." He smiled and gazed at Mona, who blushed a little.

I spoke up quickly before they went at it on the table. "Sheila told me you weren't exactly a willing participant in that. I thought Mona was controlling you."

Mona forced a nervous chuckle. "It's not quite that easy."

"I don't remember agreeing to blow up Pennsylvania," Rett countered. "The Flyers had a good team that year!"

"All I did was suggest things! You wouldn't have let the core overheat if you hadn't agreed with me on some level."

"Mona, when we were in bed, I would have agreed to campaign for Reagan—or worse, cheer for the Rangers. I'd have agreed with anything you said just to keep you there ten more minutes."

Mona turned away and got very interested in the view outside the window, where a passing cloud obscured the bright morning sun.

"When I was working there, I became very concerned about the safety at the plant. We were doing all we could to keep things under control, but it was easy to see how many corners had been cut. It was held together with duct tape. That's not an exaggeration—I saw cracks patched with actual duct tape. I told Mona how worried I was that something terrible was going to happen. And something did! I just had no idea that I would be the cause of it."

Mona shook her head vigorously. "You weren't the cause of it. Neither was I! We didn't create a meltdown."

"No, but I was the one who ignored the readings, thanks to you." He paused for more coffee. "They had an investigation and decided that the control panel was faulty. I think they'd rather say that than have to admit their employees were incompetent or actively sabotaging the place. They convinced me to take administrative leave. Fully paid, of course. Which was fine with me. I was ready to quit anyway. There was no way I could stay there."

Rett slumped forward in his chair. The memory seemed to deflate him. "I felt terrible about everything. I spent a lot of time drinking and feeling sorry for myself. One night, I woke up in a church mission. I had no idea how I'd gotten there. I was hungover and feeling guilty as hell. A priest asked me what was wrong, and I started to cry. Just poured everything out of me and onto him. I told him how I'd almost hurt thousands of people and could never make that right. He told me that God can forgive anyone, as long as the sinner is contrite and willing to make amends. He offered me a hand, and the next thing I know, I'm helping him dole out soup in the breadline. I worked with him for a few months and then entered the seminary. I was ordained not long after that."

"It doesn't sound like you parted with Mona on great terms," I said.

"I didn't." He glared at Mona until she squirmed in her seat. "I was furious at her for what she did. I let her know it too. I told her I felt betrayed. She just said that her work was too important to let puppy love get in the way and that I'd understand one day."

Sheila smiled. "That sounds familiar."

Mona frowned at her.

"And yet," I said, "here we are."

Rett nodded. "Turns out, she was right."

Mona smiled.

"It was long after I'd been asked to leave the church. I was trying to preach in my new ministry. I had heard about a nuclear protest in Indian Point, New York. I headed there to help spread the word." He gestured to the camper around us. "I pulled up in the portable chapel here, and who do you think was out front and chained to the gate?" He reached over and rubbed Mona's shoulder. "They had to take the whole gate off the hinges. They called in the National Guard! It was glorious. She almost didn't recognize me when I bailed her out. She was so surprised to see me, she was speechless."

I glanced at Sheila, and we both had to suppress a laugh. That must have been something.

"Anyway, once I got her out of jail, we caught up on old times. It was funny; we both started by trying to apologize to each other, if you can believe it!"

"No," Sheila said. "I can't."

Mona ignored that. "I tried to tell him I was sorry for tricking him at the plant."

"And I told her I was sorry for doubting her. I may not have liked all her methods, but I agreed with what she was trying to do. Every day, we do more damage to what God left for us to watch over. Every day, we get one step closer to a precipice. Soon, we'll step over, and there will be no going back. Since then, Mona and I have kept in touch."

Mona laughed. "That's one way to put it."

Rett laughed too. "Anyway, she emailed me about the pulp plant a few years ago, and I made my way up here to help out however I could."

"Is that when you met Caleb?" I asked.

"Oh no. I met him long before that. In the early nineties, I was traveling to college campuses all over. Clinton had energized a lot of students, and there was a sense that things might really change." Rett sighed. "It was nice while it lasted, before he turned out to be a corporate whore like all the rest. But, for a while, there was real electricity in the air. So many people wanted to make a difference. And Caleb was one of them."

Rett refilled his cup and had a sip. "Right away, I saw he was different. I had set up shop on the street just outside the campus at the University of Southern Maine in Portland when he came up to me. His eyes can cut right through you, you know?"

I did. I shuddered a little, thinking about him in the diner, how his eyes went from kind to cold glass in a heartbeat.

"He wanted to save the earth, but he felt the other students weren't really serious, just trying to get laid. He was tired of playing games and wanted to do something that mattered. I was thrilled. I told him we always need men of action. That suited him fine. He wanted to know everything. And not just the basic stuff about ice caps. He wanted to know about tactics. How to organize. How to infiltrate."

I perked up at that. "Like how to break into a chemical plant without getting caught?"

Rett grinned from ear to ear. "I can neither confirm nor deny. Anyway, I was packing up to leave at the end of the week when Caleb came by with a backpack. He wanted to come with me. Said I'd taught him more in four days than college had in two years. Well, it can get a bit dull on the road with no one to talk to, so I said sure." He pointed at where I was sitting. "Right there was where he rolled out his sleeping bag. He barely even snored."

I had seen how people reacted to Caleb when he turned on the charm. "I'll bet that he was a great travel companion. At first."

Rett smiled. "You got it. Top shelf, by the glove hand. He was great at first. Paid for gas. Helped with the driving. And he could cook a mean engine-block-grilled salmon."

Orson lifted his head when he heard *salmon*, but then he drifted back to sleep.

"He stayed with me for two years, in fact. We went to a bunch of protests, caused a lot of trouble." Rett sighed. "But in the end, we really didn't stop that much."

Mona clucked in sympathy. "I know the feeling. You try and try to get the word out, but the damn corporate press just ignores you or treats you like you're crazy. Then the plant gets built or the forest gets uprooted, and people wonder why the cancer rate spikes."

Rett nodded. "I'd been at it a while by that point. I knew that for every construction project you stop, or even delay, twenty more go on as if you said nothing. I'm used to it. I savor my victories. Caleb... well, patience was never his strong suit."

Sheila looked at the spot on the floor where Caleb used to sleep. "What finally made him leave?"

"We had come from a fracking protest. At the time, it was a pretty new development. The energy companies had figured out how to get at all the natural gas right under their feet in the Northeast. We tried to tell them how bad this would be for the water table, but no one wanted to listen, not when the energy companies were literally throwing money at everyone. Caleb could accept that some people didn't think about the forests or wildlife, but water? Who didn't need water? He absolutely refused to believe it. He started shouting at me about how I was just another sellout and how we needed to take more direct actions. The way he was gritting his teeth, I could guess what he meant. I tried to tell him that it was a bad idea. People could get hurt—innocent people. 'No one who hurts our world is innocent,' he said. I tried to tell him about the consequences, about the guilt I felt after Three Mile Island."

Mona gasped. "Did you tell him about me?"

Rett shook his head. "No, I never mentioned your name. I did tell him what had happened and how I'd been 'persuaded,' but I never said by who. But after that, Caleb was a man possessed. No more passive resistance for him. The fracking operation had started up. We'd tried to stop them, but it was no use. After we'd lost that last battle, Caleb up and left. He couldn't take any more defeats." Rett pushed himself away from the tiny table. "Come on outside. I need to show you this."

We shuffled and scooted around the cramped trailer and made our way out the door. Orson grunted his displeasure with having to move.

Rett gathered us around the front of his pickup. "I was settling down for the night in a campground near the drill site. I'd been followed by some locals who weren't too happy about us trying to stop the operation and the checks they were getting. They were shouting at me, calling me every name in the book." He counted them off on his fingers. "Tree hugger, hippie, fag—all the classics. The camp owner had to call a trooper in when they started to throw rocks at my trailer." He pointed at a huge dent on the hood. "That one was from a brick." He then pointed at the mangled front fender. "That was a cinder block. It was right then that there was a huge explosion. The night was lit up with fire. I looked up and saw the hillside was burning."

Sheila guessed. "It was Caleb."

Rett nodded. "He'd stolen some dynamite from the work site and planted it in the drilling room. The few sticks of dynamite shouldn't have done that much damage, but they must have mixed with the natural gas. The plant was a crater. Three people died."

I stomped my feet to keep warm. Mona rubbed her arms. It was freezing out, but the chill was coming from Rett's story.

Rett sat on the hood of the truck, nestling into the dent from the brick. "In a way, I was lucky those people were trying to kill me. Because the cop was there and there were so many witnesses, they couldn't pin it on me. Believe me, they wanted to. I told them about Caleb and then got out of town before they changed their minds and decided to lock me up just to be safe. But Caleb was long gone. I haven't seen him since."

Sheila exhaled slowly through her nose, little tendrils of steam curling around her head. "So he's always been passionate about the environment, but the magic is new."

Rett nodded. "I don't know where he learned that. He was always very interested in native traditions, but while I knew him, he never did anything like the stuff Mona's told me about."

"So when did he figure that out?" I asked.

No one had an answer for that.

"We have to call the police. If he's threatening to blow up the plant, we have to warn them. Even if they don't believe it."

Sheila shook her head. "We saw what they can do. That plant won't stand a chance, but the cops won't do much, either."

Rett nodded. "I don't have a phone here. No reception in the woods where I usually go." He hopped off the hood, went to the passenger door, and pulled a battered road atlas out of the cab. "There's a town not too far from here. I can lead you to it."

Mona sighed in resignation. "It won't do any good. They won't listen."

Sheila frowned. "Well, what then? Just let it blow up?"

Stop them. Orson yipped from beside my feet. *We have to stop them.*

Sheila reached down to pet his head. "Baby, that's sweet. But I can't let him hurt you again."

He made me hurt Gabe. He made me hurt the pack. Orson growled and whined. *He doesn't get away with that.*

That hung in the air a minute, then I said, "Orson, I forgave you. Don't get yourself hurt for that."

Not me. He won't hurt anyone else.

Mona clucked. "He's a very brave dog." She looked at Sheila. "I know where he gets it from."

Sheila blushed then shook her head. "You saw that thing. We could barely slow it down. Caleb is one thing, but how are we supposed to stop that?"

"I don't know, dear, but I know we can't let him roam free. Who knows how much damage he could do, especially if he can teach his disciples how to do... that?"

Rett agreed. "He could be scary without magic. If he can assume some kind of demonic form, then all bets are off."

Sheila glanced to me, and I took her hand. "Babe, you know I'll follow you anywhere. I'll always be with you." I nudged Orson with my foot. "You, too, buddy. If you want to take a stand, I'm here to help."

"No, you weren't there. You don't understand what it was like to see him like that."

"I *was* there! Our car has a giant dent in it, thanks to that thing."

She shook her head. "It's not the same. It was worse seeing him change like that in person."

I held her tighter. "I know that if it frightened you, it must be terrible. But you aren't alone. I'm here. Orson's here. Mona can help. And Rett knows all about him. Plus, I get the feeling he's not one to leave something alone when he gets his mind set about it. If he thinks we could be a problem, then he's going to make things hard for us."

Sheila sighed. "You're right. He won't leave us alone. Any of us. But I can't let you get hurt, and we don't know how to stop him." She frowned. "Not that it matters. If his letter wasn't just an idle threat, today's the day he intends to bring down the factory. We're out of time."

Rett chimed in. "What was the word he used? 'Kisulk'?"

Mona nodded. "Yes. It's from the native legends—"

"Of the creator spirit, right." Rett finished the thought for her. "Maybe we need someone to tell us more about that. Let us know what we're up against." Rett ran over to the driver's side with a burst of energy. "I know just the place! Follow me in your car. We'll be there in no time!" He leapt into the cab of the pickup and cranked the engine. He leaned out the window. "Hop in, Mona! We can catch up on the way."

Mona tossed me her keys. "I'll ride with him. If he gets too far ahead, I can let you know where we're going. Besides, you heard him. We've got some catching up to do." She winked at us and got into the passenger seat of the battered pickup. She had barely closed the door when the car and trailer started with a lurch and headed down the road.

I walked over to Mona's boxy little car and opened the door. Sheila was still standing in the clearing where the trailer had been moments ago. Orson paced by her feet.

She sighed deeply. "We could still just go, you know. We could turn around, head back to Caribou, pick up the car, and leave town. Once we got far enough away, you could call the FBI and leave an anonymous tip. We don't have to go down this rabbit hole and fight these people with my crazy aunt."

I walked over to her and put my hand on her shoulder. "Yes, we could. We could drive back south and maybe even go to Mexico or California. Somewhere nice and warm."

Sheila snuggled up to me.

"But..."

She exhaled into my chest. "But if we don't help, everyone in that plant is as good as dead. And Mona can't handle it on her own. I can't let my aunt die. She's all the family I have."

Orson gave a sad bark. Sheila laughed. "I meant besides the two of you." She hugged me and started back toward the car. "Come on. We need to get after them before they get too far ahead."

EIGHTEEN

I tried to keep the camper van in sight. That wasn't hard since there was only one road. Lined with snow-covered pine trees, it seemed to stretch on forever. Sheila leaned her head against the window and shut her eyes. She groaned each time the car hit a bump. She groaned a lot.

We had spent about thirty minutes lurching and bumping, cursing the Samurai's nonexistent suspension, when Orson barked. *Bunny!* He tried to wedge himself between the seats, tongue lolling out happily. Indeed, there was a little gray bunny perched in the snow on the left side of the road. I nudged Sheila. She peeked out through barely open eyes and gave Orson a scratch.

"Yes, bunny. Let Mama rest, okay?" She closed her eyes and tried to nap.

Orson panted some more then barked again with pleasure. *Bunny!*

A different one, a brown one, sat a hundred feet farther down the road.

Sheila looked puzzled. "Don't bunnies hibernate?"

I shrugged. "I didn't stick with the Boy Scouts long enough to find out." Six raccoons had come out of the woods on the right side and sat up on their haunches, watching our car go by. "I am pretty sure that raccoons are nocturnal, though."

Orson bobbed his head from side to side. He loved to chase things. His happy smile faded away. *That's a lot of bunnies.*

I tried to glance over while avoiding the craters and potholes, but then I couldn't look away. Lining both sides of the road, shoulder to shoulder, were rows of wildlife. Rabbits, raccoons, and squirrels. Crows and blue jays started to settle in the trees along our route. It began to look like a scene from a low-budget Noah's Ark movie. Tree branches started to sag under the weight of the wildlife.

I grabbed Sheila's leg. "Are you seeing this? Is Mona?"

Sheila nodded. "She is, and she doesn't like it, either. It seems like Caleb's trying to show that he can keep an eye on us."

I remembered the birds and bears we encountered yesterday. "I hope that's all it is. I don't think this tin can we're in could stand getting hit by a moose or a deer." Almost on cue, I saw antlers poke out from behind the line of critters. A couple of deer and a moose. I thought I saw a ripple of black fur also.

I tightened my grip on the wheel. "Tell her to step on it."

Sheila nodded. Ahead of us, the camper van lurched forward.

I stomped on the gas pedal to keep up, but the Samurai had almost no acceleration. It sped up gradually until we matched pace with Rett and Mona. "How much longer? I want to get off this road ASAP."

Sheila stared at the camper for a second. "Mona says it's not far, but this is the only road."

My mouth had suddenly gotten very dry. I swallowed. I'd never thought bunnies and squirrels could be menacing, but there were a lot of things I'd never thought before that were becoming all too real. It seemed as if they were fidgeting, straining against a wall that they were about to burst through.

And then they did. Hundreds of creatures flooded into the road. They swarmed toward us. I gunned the car as much as I could, and Rett did the same ahead of us. We bounced through some giant potholes and went airborne, landing with a thud. My head banged into the roof, and I promised myself that I would only drive on four-lane highways from then on—if we ever got back to one.

Fortunately, even our ragtag convoy could outpace most of the woodland army. Several deer were managing to keep up with us, though. I could see their glassy eyes as they sprinted alongside the windows of the car. I tried to go faster, but the Samurai was topping out at forty. That was all she could handle on the terrible road. I heard a thunk as a doe banged her head into the side window. Orson barked madly. Then antlers scraped across the passenger side.

Sheila gasped and gripped her armrest. "Mona says we just have to hang on. We're almost there."

I heard a few more thumps from behind me but didn't look back. "How far?"

Suddenly, the deer skidded to a halt. The birds veered away, and the critters stumbled to a stop. We drove on, but they had stopped as if they'd run into a force field.

Orson whined. *What happened?*

I looked ahead and saw a sign: NOW ENTERING PENOB-SCOT NATION TRIBAL TERRITORY.

"Maybe we found something Caleb can't handle." I glanced behind me. The birds had dispersed, but a couple were still making lazy loops in the sky.

Not long after the animals dropped away, we came to a small town in the middle of nowhere. Calling it a "town" might have been pushing it, though. There was a gas pump outside of a general store at a crossroads with a few run-down houses scattered around. Rett pulled the camper over to the pump and hopped out. He stretched and jogged into the store.

"Is this where we were going?" I asked, "Or does he just have to pee?"

Sheila closed her eyes for a moment. "Mona says we're here. Wherever that is." She kept her eyes closed as she pulled her coat around her neck and stepped out into the cold Maine air. Orson scrabbled out from the cramped back seat and flopped into the snow. He grunted and whined sadly as he shook the snow out of the crevasses on his face.

Mona stepped out of Rett's truck. She cracked her neck and trudged over to us.

"Where are we?" I asked.

Mona shrugged. "I'm not one hundred percent sure. It's a Penobscot territory. I know that much. About twenty-five miles northwest of where Rett was camped out, which was about fifty miles west of my house."

"So how about eighty percent?"

Mona rubbed a kink out of her neck. "From what I could guess, we're somewhere near Allagash. It's the northwest tip of the state, right next to Quebec."

Ooh la la! Let's get some poutine!

I glanced down at the shivering dog. "How do you even know what poutine is?"

It was on the Cooking Channel.

Mona hooted. "They probably don't have that here, but let's get inside anyway. Get out of the cold."

Sheila didn't say anything, but she gave me a brief nod before we headed into the run-down little convenience store. The shelves held a small selection of snack foods and canned goods. Miraculously, there was a pay phone in the back next to a grimy bathroom door flanked by shelves of motor oil and wiper fluid.

Trying to find a phone was always frustrating. Sheila hated cell phones. Her last coven had made her extremely paranoid about them since their priestess was convinced people were out to get them. In this case, I was in total agreement. I preferred the Maine police not have any traceable link to me.

I pointed the phone out to Sheila. "I'm going to call and warn them." I fished around in my pocket for coins as I made my way back. The old phone had a rotary dial, and I hoped it worked. The crackly dial tone was a relief. Cradling the cold plastic handset against my shoulder, I realized I didn't have a number for the Caribou police, so I spun the zero for the operator. It clicked slowly back into place and—astonishingly—the line started to ring. And ring.

Finally, an operator picked up. "AT&T. How may I help you?"

"Yeah, can you connect me to the police department in Caribou, Maine?"

"Yes, sir. That will be fifty cents plus a call fee of—"

A large hand had reached across and pressed down on the receiver lever, ending the call. I looked to my left and saw a very angry native man. At least six feet tall, he was built like a linebacker and had jet-black hair in a shoulder-length ponytail. He was scowling at me. "And why does this white boy want to call the police so badly?"

I stammered for a second until Rett came out of the bathroom, wiping his hands on a paper towel. "Hey, Chief! Aw, don't mess with him. He's cool."

The big man gave me the stink eye for a moment longer then broke into a huge smile. "Rett! Good to see you!" He shook Rett's hand vigorously then pulled him into a bear hug.

Rett grinned and turned to me. "Meet Johnny Orono. He's a descendant of Joseph Orono, one of the greatest chiefs the Penobscot Nation ever had."

Johnny grinned. "Yeah, well, I'm not chief of anything but this magnificent gaseteria." He gestured to the surrounding shelves, where I thought I saw a can of dusty Spam with an expiration date from the nineties. "But you didn't answer the question." Johnny's grin faded away. "Why are you trying to call the police? We have enough trouble with those assholes."

Rett matched his frown. "It's not like that. It's about our old buddy Caleb."

Johnny's eyes flared with anger. "That fucker?" He turned to me. "Go ahead and call. And tell the cops to shoot him on sight."

I nodded my thanks and picked up the phone again. It took fifty cents to connect to Caribou and another fifty to keep the line open while I got bounced around and put on hold. Finally, the desk sergeant spoke to me.

"Caribou Police. How may we protect and serve you today?" He sounded like I'd caught him mid coffee break, as he spoke around something in his mouth.

"Listen to me," I said. "Someone is going to attack the paper mill."

"What?"

"That weirdo in the antlers. The one from the groundbreaking. He's back, and he's going to destroy the mill. You have to get the people out of there."

"Yeah, right. The only weirdo around here is that crazy bat Mona that lives out in the woods."

I sighed. I knew this was going to be a bust, but we had to try. "Look, I don't care if you don't believe me. Something destroyed Mona's house last night, and they're moving on to the mill today. Go check it out. Just please get the workers out of harm's way."

I could practically hear him rolling his eyes. "Yeah, we'll get right on that." And he hung up.

Sheila walked up to me as I put down the phone. "How did it go?"

I shrugged. "About as well as I expected."

Sheila grimaced.

"Maybe they'll send a cruiser by the mill, but I doubt they'll do more than that."

She sighed. "Then we have to go back."

I nodded and looked to the front of the store. Mona, Rett, and Johnny were laughing and smiling, catching up on old times. Mona caught my eye midlaugh. I shook my head, and the smile faded away.

"No go with the cops?"

I shook my head. "They're convinced the only weirdo in the area is you. We have to go back and stop Caleb before innocent people get hurt."

Mona nodded. "We'd better get going." She turned to the door, but Sheila stopped her.

"If Caleb succeeds and you're anywhere near the plant when it gets destroyed, the cops will arrest you without a second thought."

"Sweetie, if we work together, there's no way he can—"

Sheila cut her off. "We don't know how strong he is. We saw him playing with animals from miles away." She looked away from Mona's eyes. "You're the only relative I have, and I don't want you getting blamed for this."

She reached over and drew Sheila into a hug. After a few seconds, Mona found her voice. "All right. I'll wait here with Rett. Let me know the minute you stop him."

Sheila nodded. I shook Rett's hand, then Sheila, Orson, and I piled back into the Samurai and drove off, back to Caribou.

NINETEEN

We bounced along the back roads as fast as we dared. Mona's Samurai whined and strained, but it couldn't get much above fifty. Our fear of yet more animal attacks didn't help, either. We jumped in our seats every time Orson barked at a squirrel. We had been on the road a couple of hours, and the sun was already starting its descent.

"Do you think we'll make it in time?" I asked.

Sheila had a bitter frown on her face. "Of course. He's not going to do anything until we show up. He wants to prove how strong he is and crush us in the process."

I didn't feel particularly relieved at that.

As we got close to the outskirts of town and the paper mill, Sheila fished a ring out of a small pouch that hung off her belt. Its purple stone was a chip off the larger one buried underneath Wendy's shop. Yareth, a crazy lovelorn wizard, had broken off a chunk and set it in a tacky ring to make it a little more portable. Sheila had almost tossed it in with the larger stone, but Wendy had convinced her to hang on to it. That seemed like a brilliant idea at the moment. The stone had the effect of boosting a witch's abilities, and we were without Mona.

Sheila frowned. She hadn't touched the stone since Florida. "I hate the way that stone made me feel." That was understandable.

"If you don't feel comfortable, then don't use it. You, me, and Orson will be enough to clear out the plant."

Her frown became a rueful smile. "That's just it. It felt way too comfortable. Like nothing ever felt better." She held the ring by the band and examined the stone. "This is much smaller than that rock. And we'll need all the help we can get to deal with him." She took a breath then slid it onto her finger. She closed her eyes and shivered. When she opened them again, her irises were tinged with purple.

She grinned at me. "Let's do this."

We arrived at the pulp mill shortly after four. The sun was already starting to set, but the lot was still full of older model cars and pickups. The mill was still standing, so either Caleb had been bluffing all along, or he hadn't arrived yet. Or Sheila was right, and he was just waiting for us to show up.

No cops. They hadn't believed me. *What a surprise.*

We stopped just outside the lot and piled out of the tiny car.

Sheila looked at the building in front of us. "So... shall we go inside?"

I shrugged. "Sure. At the very least, we can pull the fire alarm and get people out." That wasn't a felony, unlike a fake bomb threat.

We headed inside the lot. There was one guard at an entrance booth, reading a paperback. Sheila didn't even need to use magic to distract him. We jogged up the main drive to the building. Smoke was belching out of the stacks with that distinctive smell permeating the lot. Production was in full swing. We burst through the main door. The secretary at the reception desk looked up as the door flung open. Sheila's eyes flashed gold, and the woman looked back down, ignoring us.

Sheila stood between the door and the reception desk. I searched the walls for a fire alarm and saw one behind the receptionist. I dashed over to pull it, then I felt something crawling around the back of my head.

Hello, Gabriel. Glad you finally decided to show up.

Sheila was right. Caleb had been waiting for us. *Damn it.* I reached forward to pull the alarm—at least I tried to. It seemed that my hand was stuck about two inches away from the lever.

Ah, ah, ah. That would spoil all the fun.

I tried to call Sheila, but my voice didn't want to work, either. I tried to turn my head to her, but the best I could do was peek out the side of my eye. Sheila wasn't looking at me. She was staring out the glass door at the front. I could guess what she was looking at—a bunch of nature freaks in loincloths and one in antlers.

It's too bad that Mona didn't come. I could have finished all of you off. At least I'll have the fun of seeing her blamed for this.

There was a rumble from deep within the structure. Caleb was starting to do his thing. I was still frozen in place. Either Sheila hadn't noticed, or she needed all her energy to keep the building from falling down around us. Footsteps moved away from me, and I heard a gasp.

"What... What the hell?" The receptionist had an entirely rational reaction.

Sheila answered calmly. "You need to evacuate the building. Right now. Pull the fire alarm, get on the intercom, get everyone out. Those lunatics intend to destroy this place."

Either magic or Sheila's powers of persuasion convinced the woman. I heard steps behind me then a shriek from the receptionist. "What are you doing? Pull the alarm!"

I tried to respond, but a strained grunt was all I could manage.

That must have gotten Sheila's attention, because I felt her hand on my shoulder. Out of the corner of my eye, I could see the glow of her ring. My shoulders slumped. I could move again. Before Caleb realized he'd lost control of me, I reached out and slammed the fire alarm.

The building had a new alarm system. Instead of the classic, high-pitched clanging, the alarm was an electronic whoop with blue strobing lights. Sheila's ring flared, and Orson growled behind me as he kept watch on the door. Deep in the building, machines shuddered to a halt. Office workers pooled into the front of the room, all stopping by the door.

"What's going on?" An office worker in a white shirt and red tie stopped next to Sheila at the door.

"There's an emergency. We have to get out now." I waved them toward the door.

"Hey, I know those freaks!" He peered out the door. "They were at the groundbreaking with that crazy old hippie. What are they doing here?"

"Sir, you have to get out now," I urged. "They called in a bomb threat." There was a rumble, and the building shuddered around us.

His eyes widened, then he raced to the door, pushing Sheila to the side, and slammed into it. He pushed and pulled frantically, but the door did not budge.

Sheila stood her ground near the entrance as best she could while more and more workers clumped around the door. Sweat started to bead on her brow. She was using all of her energy to keep the building up around us, so she couldn't deal with whatever Caleb had done to the front door. Orson whined next to me.

I pointed to Sheila. "Go help her! You know she's strong when you're with her!"

Orson stared at the ground but didn't move.

"What is it?"

I can't let him use me again.

I knelt next to him. "I know. But I know you won't let that happen. And Mama will protect you. Now go help her."

Orson nodded and started to trot over to Sheila. He nuzzled up to her leg, and Sheila's shoulders relaxed a bit. More workers flooded into the lobby. I wondered if there were back doors or loading docks. Maybe they were stuck closed too. People started to crush against the door.

After more rumbling, the ground shook again. It wouldn't take much to turn the situation into a stampede. Someone slammed into my back, and I nearly went down. Fortunately, the shoulders of the guy ahead of me broke my fall.

Cracks were appearing in the ceiling, and plaster started to fall on my head. I tried to dodge a chunk of it, but I was pinned down. The workers had plowed into the lobby, and we were packed in. A piece of ceiling tile landed right on my head, and I could barely shake it off.

The panic around me filled the room. Then the murmurs turned into screams. The chaos would turn into a riot soon, if the roof didn't collapse and crush us first.

For all my complaining about Sheila being in my head too much recently, I was desperate that she hear me right then. *Come on, Sheila. You can do it. And please do it now.* I wheezed as someone else hit the pile of people, knocking the wind out of me.

I could see Sheila's black hair through the bouncing and bobbing of the crowd. A big guy in a hard hat tried to push past her and bumped into her hard. Orson yelped as she almost fell over, but she grabbed the door handle in time to keep herself upright. I tried to move to her, but I was trapped by the mob.

I caught glimpses of her as the building shuddered. Her brow was furrowed, straining against what Caleb was throwing at her. Something was different. He'd somehow gotten so much stronger overnight.

Sheila started to sweat. I caught flashes of purple as the ring on her finger glowed. At the cottage, she and Mona had no problem dealing with Caleb and his pals, but it was suddenly much harder. Mona was gone, but Orson was working with her and not biting me on the—

That's it! When she thought I was in danger and that she needed to save me, she had lashed out with all her strength. I wondered if she was holding back, afraid of how strong she could be.

I wobbled with another shove in the back. The panic around me was palpable. People were screaming, yelling, and pushing. I had a very dangerous thought. *Orson! Sheila! Help me!*

I slumped down, tucked my head into my chest, and wrapped my arms around my knees. *Help me, Sheila!*

Sheila and Orson could usually hear me call them, but other things demanded their attention right then. I grunted as someone wearing work boots kicked me in the ribs. Maybe I should have thought this through, but we would all be dead if Sheila couldn't break Caleb's hold on the door.

Bodies slammed into me from every side, and I toppled over. Curled up on the ground, I tried to protect my head from accidental stomps. Some of them felt intentional. Feeling a boot in my back near my kidneys, I cried out in pain.

Above the din of the crowd, I heard Orson yelp. I hoped it was because he'd heard me and not because he was getting stepped on too. I then heard a gasp. Really, I felt it deep inside me. *Sheila.*

Then I definitely heard a scream of rage. Sheila. A flash of purple filled the lobby, followed by a crack, like a rib being torn out of someone's chest. A gust of cold air filled the room. I took that to mean that Sheila had managed to open the door. The crush of people around me lessened. Finally, enough people had exited that I could get up.

I took a step and almost fell down again. Orson's bite from the previous night and a couple of good stomps on the same ankle made walking a challenge.

Sheila turned her head and glared daggers at me. "You bastard... You push too hard. Get outside... I can't hold him off much longer." Even though it was twenty degrees outside, sweat rolled down her face.

I moved to the door—well, where the door had been—avoiding the ceiling tiles and plaster crashing down around me. I stepped over the threshold and turned back. Sheila and Orson both had their eyes shut tight.

"Come on, let's go!" I shouted.

I didn't hear an answer—thought or spoken. I moved to grab them, but I had barely lifted my foot off the ground when their eyes shot open. Two pairs of eyes stared at me angrily, glowing purple and gold. Orson growled, and Sheila barely whispered, "Go."

I was frozen in place, not wanting to leave her there but knowing there wasn't anything else I could do. Then I felt myself flung backward into a snowbank. Twice in two days. It was not something I wanted to get into a habit of doing. I craned my head up and saw Caleb and his followers standing in a line at the edge of the parking lot. Caleb was backlit by the setting sun, silhouetting him in a pink glow. Then, theatrically, he raised his hand and closed it into a fist.

I turned back to the factory. My love and her dog were standing in the hole of the doorway. Then the factory crumpled around them, like a paper cup being crushed in an angry fist.

TWENTY

My mouth dropped open. I tried to scream, but nothing came out. The rumble of destruction that echoed through the quiet Maine forest had swallowed the sound. Cinder block and brick rained down as the building crumpled. With an unnatural crack, the bulk of the mill fell into the hole of the foundation pit, as if being swallowed up. A thick cloud of dust and debris swirled above it. There was still no sign of Sheila or Orson. I searched for them with my mind, frantically casting out, but I couldn't hear anything.

I couldn't believe what I'd seen. Sheila had easily stopped Caleb at Mona's cottage, but he'd just crumpled an enormous processing plant like cardboard. How strong was he?

I turned my head slowly and saw Caleb, antler hoodie and all, striding to the ruins of the plant. He still appeared to be human and not the unholy bone monster. The employees who had run outside scattered as Caleb strode past them. One brave and foolhardy man tried to step up to him. The burly man ran up to Caleb and screamed, "Hey, asshole! What the fuck do you think you're—"

Caleb swatted the air with the barest flick of his hand, as if he were lazily swatting at a moth. The big guy went flying. He slammed into the side of a sedan in the parking lot then slumped down, leaving a head-shaped dent in the door panel. I hoped he was just unconscious.

Caleb stalked forward with purpose, decidedly unhurried. Someone must have called the cops already. Even with their established record of not giving a damn, the cops had to be arriving soon. Caleb didn't seem to care, though.

His helpers trailed after him. I counted eight people in loincloths. Some of them exchanged glances, looking a bit shocked. They could join the club. I'd seen a lot of things in the past couple years, and the mill's implosion was still off-the-charts insane.

Caleb stopped at the edge of the pit. The crumpled factory walls were heaped in piles. He pointed down into the pit. Slowly, gingerly, the loincloth brigade slid down into the frozen dirt. He stood watch, arms crossed, and waited, with that stupid deer skull on his head.

I wanted to charge at him, but he'd already shown that he could get in my head without a problem. And even if he was distracted enough to let me get near, he could still swat me aside like the big guy with a concussion in the parking lot.

It would have been more prudent to watch and see what he was after, but I was not in a prudent state of mind right then. And if he had hurt Sheila or Orson, I would get revenge or die trying.

I rolled onto my stomach and got up on my haunches to test the pressure on my legs. I winced. The bruises Orson had given me were getting tight and the new ones I'd just gotten were starting to set. Though I had no idea how fast I would be able to move, I was not going to just let that asshole walk away. I pulled my blackjack out of the inner pocket of my coat. The leather-handled miniclub I always carried with me had gotten me out of a lot of tight spots before. I hoped it could get me through one more.

I took a baby step forward to adjust my weight. Caleb was yelling at the people in the hole and pointing. He was about twenty yards away and had his back to me. If I was going to do anything, it'd better be now.

I lurched to my feet and started running toward Caleb. I was not nearly as fast as I would have liked, but I only had to cover about twenty strides before he saw me.

I was halfway there, and he hadn't noticed me. After five more steps, he heard me. After two more, he started to turn. I leapt at him. I caught him in the side, and we tumbled into the pit. We rolled down the hill a few feet until we got to the lip. We went over a sudden drop-off where a basement room must have been, and after dropping a few feet, we landed on the dirt with a thud. Fortunately, I landed on top, so I was only a little winded. Caleb groaned loudly under my weight. I guess my road food diet had at least one benefit.

Caleb moaned and tried to stand. That snapped me back to the present. Before he could get it together, I levered myself up and started whacking at his skull crest with my blackjack. I got in a few good ones and managed to crack the bone. If Caleb wasn't hulking out, then I was dealing with plain old bone and not an invulnerable magic monster. Maybe that would apply to the man inside the skull too. Caleb tried to get his arms up and managed to block a few of my swings. He was a pretty strong guy even without magical help. I was about to swing down again when something grabbed my right arm on the backswing.

Two of Caleb's helpers, young men with dark hair that reached the back of their necks, had dropped into the hole. Oddly, they weren't shivering in their loincloths. Since they were hanging on to my right arm, I turned to punch with my left. With a solid crunch, the first kid fell over and grabbed at his nose. The other's eyes popped wide—right before I socked him in the jaw.

The kids were down, but that was all the distraction Caleb had needed. I caught a glimpse of a red-purple glow deep in the eyes of the skull, then I felt myself flying into the wall. I slumped down next to the two moaning kids, ready to call it a day myself. My vision blurred as I saw Caleb stand up. From down on the cold floor, he looked about seven feet tall. He looked down at me and smiled wickedly.

"Nice try, but not nearly good enough." He raised his hands, probably about to bring another building down on me.

I closed my eyes. Then I heard a loud crash but didn't feel anything. I opened my eyes tentatively. Sheila was on top of the pit wall. Her eyes were on fire, and she was sending a shower of bricks down on Caleb. Orson barked angrily next to her. They were both covered in dust and concrete crumbs.

Caleb bent over to shield himself from the onslaught. He grabbed the two young men, one in each hand, and I could have sworn he winked at me. "Next time."

He grinned. Then, with only one running step, he leapt out of the six-foot hole and onto the ground. The rest of them scurried away, and I heard Sheila and Orson chase them off.

I sat on the ground, rubbing my head. My eyes had uncrossed, so I hoped I wasn't concussed. I tried to stand up and drag myself out of the hole. As I got onto my knees, I saw something on the ground.

Right where the two guys had fallen over, I found two tiny transparent crystals carved to look like people. They were a little larger than gummy bears and very detailed, each of them finely carved to showcase the curve of a chin and the musculature of chest and legs. I hadn't noticed them on the basement floor, so they must have come from Caleb's people or fallen in from the outside. I tried to pick them up and yelped. They were so cold, colder than they could have possibly been, even after lying outside in the Maine winter. My fingertips felt frostbitten where I'd touched them. I fished a pair of gloves out of my coat pocket and used one to scoop the stones into the other. I could still feel them radiating iciness through the gloves and my pocket.

After that, I heaved myself out of the pit with a lot of panting. Once out, I saw Sheila and Orson waiting for me. And Sheila was not happy.

TWENTY-ONE

"**S**heila, thank God you're all right!" I went in to hold her, but she stepped back and held up her hand.

She glared at me. "What the fuck was that stunt you pulled at the plant? Were you trying to get killed?"

I was a little taken aback. "You're mad about *that*? Caleb just dropped a building on you, and that's your first question?"

"Of course. I can handle myself. What I can't handle is you doing something stupid."

Orson whined and scratched at the ground. He could never handle it when his mama got angry.

I tried to deflect her anger. "How did you get out of there?"

She gave a dismissive wave. "I'm not new at this. I can shield myself from a lot of things, you know. I can protect myself and those I care about, provided they aren't trying to screw me up. Was that what you were doing?"

"No, of course not," I said. "It was just that you were in a stalemate with Caleb. I thought it might be enough to get you to overcome it."

Her eyes flared with rage, the golden specks in them glinting in the last rays of the sunset. "You did that on purpose? You manipulated me?" She clenched her fists.

I tried to stay calm. "When Caleb was at Mona's last night and Orson bit me, you lashed out. You knocked the house over with your power and got me out of harm's way." My logic was doing nothing to mollify her, and it was making Orson keen louder. "If I hadn't done something, the whole place would have come down on us."

"Oh, you know so much about magic now, you think you know how to push me? You don't have the first clue. I was doing fine holding him off until I had to worry about your stupid stunts."

Anger rose inside me. I used to have a temper. Sheila had helped me tame it, but she was provoking me. I was quickly forgetting everything she'd taught me.

"Oh, really? You had it all under control? That's why the doors wouldn't open and I almost got crushed by a panicked mob—because you had it all under control. It's okay to admit you needed a push, because if you *hadn't* got one, everyone in that plant would be under a ton of rubble."

Sheila's eyes went wide with shock and surprise. She stepped right up to my face, her nose practically touching mine. She opened her mouth to scream at me, but Orson bullied his way between us.

No! He barked loudly to make sure we got the message, then he growled until we were both looking at him.

Frowning, he stared up at Sheila. *Right, we had no problem holding him off. You, me, and the ring could barely keep the roof up.* Then he whipped his head at me so fast I could feel flecks of drool on my cheek. *You put your life in danger to give her a push when she already had her hands full. You could've died. Are you as dumb as you look? Of course you are. You think the Mets are a real baseball team.*

Orson barked loudly again. *What is wrong with you two? That guy tore a factory apart, and you both care more about who's the bigger jerk. You were almost crushed to death.*

I could have sworn he was about to start crying. His big, sad eyes got watery, and he turned away from us. He trotted over to the pile of rubble and sat down. Without a word, Sheila and I went over and knelt beside him. We each put an arm around him then leaned into each other.

"I'm sorry. I shouldn't have given you another thing to worry about, but the ceiling was cracking, and the room was full of people. I didn't know what else to do."

"I'm sorry," Sheila said. "I shouldn't have yelled. But Orson was right. We could barely hold off Caleb. You saw what he did. He was almost toying with us. He can do things I've never seen before, and I am frankly a little scared. Even in Florida, with that stone boosting everyone's power, I didn't think this was possible."

I struggled for something to say. "Mona did say how strong the energies were up here. Maybe it's that?"

Sheila shrugged, despondent. "I don't know. I guess it's possible. There is a lot of natural energy up here. It could explain why I've been so short-tempered lately. Sometimes these things have a way of amplifying emotions as well as abilities."

"Nah. You're just engaged to a jackass."

Got that right.

I scratched Orson on the head then picked myself up. "We'd better get going. The police will be here soon, and I don't feel like telling them 'I told you so.'" I offered Sheila a hand and pulled her to her feet. "Well, I do, but then I'd be here a lot longer trying to explain why we knew and all that."

Orson growled as he stood up. *I'd set them straight.*

Sheila giggled. "I bet you would. You can be very convincing, especially when you drool on people."

It's called diplomacy. Try it sometime.

We headed back to Mona's little beater car. Fortunately, we had left it far enough away from the plant that it was unharmed by stray chunks of the building. A few of the plant workers we passed weren't as lucky. Two guys in barn coats and work boots stood staring at the hood of their pickup. A six-foot piece of concrete and rebar had pierced the engine and pinned the vehicle to the ground. Most of the employees were standing around in scattered little clumps, stunned into silence. As we walked between them, their eyes followed us as we passed, and I heard little murmurs in our wake.

I looked over my shoulder, trying to gauge the workers and how likely they were to charge at us as I reached for the car door.

Suddenly, someone grabbed my hand. Alarmed, I turned to face whoever had managed to sneak up on me. It was one of Caleb's little helpers. A girl, barely twenty, she wore the standard uniform of loincloth and shoulder wrap. Long dark hair framed her face, and her eyes were wide and scared. Her teeth were chattering loudly, and she was shivering.

I squared off, ready to defend us in case it was some sort of trap. Orson barked and growled.

The girl held up her free hand. "Stop! P-Please, I need to t-talk to you!" She was trying to talk through the chills. Then, a moment later, I could feel her voice in my head. *Please. Please, you have to listen.*

Sheila frowned at her angrily, but after a second, she nodded. Orson stepped back from the car door, but he still growled. I opened the door for her, and she crawled into the back seat, her loincloth flapping.

Sheila rolled her eyes as she crossed to the passenger door. "Doesn't any woman in Maine wear a shirt?" Orson refused to get in the back seat with our new passenger and instead curled up in at Sheila's feet in the front footwell.

I started the car and drove away. The flicker of police lights arrived on the scene as I left the property. We headed back into the heart of Maine.

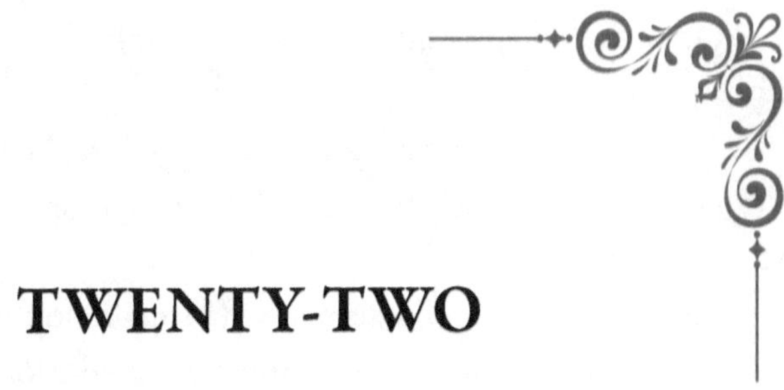

TWENTY-TWO

It would take about two hours to make our way back to Mona and Rett, and the sky was already pitch-black. There should have been stars, but I didn't see any. We rode in silence until we had gotten clear of the town. Even Orson didn't whine about being hungry.

I had cranked up the heat all the way in the Samurai, but it wasn't doing a whole lot. The girl in the back seat had wrapped herself in a dirty blanket Mona kept stashed back there, but she was still shivering violently.

Orson snorted from Sheila's feet. *Why is she cold?*

With a start, Sheila and I looked at each other. He was right. The lot of them were running around in loincloths, and the cold never seemed to bother them before. Sheila turned in her seat to look back at her. "Yeah, why are you cold?"

She shivered, barely able to get out an answer. "B-Because... I'm not with him. Not anymore."

Sheila's eyes narrowed dangerously. "You looked pretty 'with him' when he dropped a factory on us." Orson hopped up onto her lap and growled in agreement.

The girl responded by pushing herself back into the seat, as if she were trying to disappear. "I w-was. I'm not-t. Not now."

Orson barked, and she shrank back farther.

I adjusted the rearview mirror to keep an eye on her while I drove. "Maybe you'd better explain yourself. We don't like it much when people lie to us. Do we, pal?"

Orson bared all of his teeth, and a string of drool dangled from his lip.

The girl's eyes widened, and she hugged the blanket tighter around herself. "I'm not lying. I'm not with him anymore. I can't..." She started to cry into her hands.

That stopped me. I'd seen my dad make my mom cry too many times. I couldn't stand seeing women cry, and I loathed being the one causing it. Didn't matter that she was trying to kill us an hour ago. Orson stopped growling too.

Sheila let the girl cry it out for a few seconds before putting a hand on her knee. "Hey, it's going to be okay. We know what it's like to get caught up in something like this. We can help you deal with it."

I bit my tongue. The last time I'd dealt with a minion who'd been "caught up" in the web of a big bad magic guy, I'd threatened him with death until he almost peed himself. I guessed that wasn't what Sheila meant.

Orson chuffed. *Maybe not the best time to try that. Keep it in your back pocket, though.*

Fortunately, Sheila ignored us both. "Tell us what happened. Just start with your name."

The girl snuffled. Sheila handed her an almost-clean napkin that had been crammed in the ashtray. She blew her nose loudly then composed herself.

"I'm Rebecca. Rebecca Laurel. I'm, uh, I was a college student at USM in Portland."

"Hey, Rebecca. I'm Sheila, and this is Gabriel."

I gave a little wave as I navigated us around the potholes.

"And this little guy is Orson."

Orson grinned, and his tongue lolled out. Rebecca started to smile, and I felt some of her stress melt away. Orson had that effect on ladies.

"So tell me," I said, "how's a nice college girl like you end up half-naked in Caribou, blowing up pulp mills?"

Rebecca's grin faded away.

Sheila rolled her eyes. "You'll have to forgive my fiancé. He thinks he's funny."

I winked at her. "Hey, I don't think. I *know*."

"No, it's fine." She shook her head ruefully. "Now that I think about it, I can hardly believe it myself."

"Let me guess. You were an idealistic student, concerned about the environment, and you met up with someone who told you that there was something you could do about it, something better than composting. He didn't tell you what exactly. Or that it involved loincloths."

She looked at me. "Are you psychic like him?"

I stared at her in the mirror. "Look into my eyes..."

Sheila smacked me. "No. He is not. Or else he'd know not to mess around. We just heard a similar story about another young man, one you're well acquainted with, named Caleb."

Rebecca nodded. "He said that. He said he was just like me once. Full of ideals and hopes and passion. We were doing petitions on campus. We wanted the school and the state to get rid of any investments in nonrenewable energy. No oil. No fracking. No coal." She sighed. "It was slow going. I could barely get a dozen people a week to sign up. But some stupid petition to get a Dunkin' Donuts into the school cafeteria gets ten pages of signatures by lunchtime."

Orson sniffed. *Can we get a donut?*

Sheila scratched his head. "Not now, sweetie."

Rebecca looked confused. "What?"

Sheila was surprised. "You didn't hear him?"

"Who? The dog?"

Sheila looked at me. "I guess she's not so magically strong without Caleb."

Rebecca looked sullen. "No. That's for sure. He was so powerful. And so convincing." She sighed, sounding almost wistful. "People were listening to us. People were *afraid* of us. Do you get that? Years of being called a dumb hippie and being laughed at because I didn't want the planet to turn into a Mad Max wasteland, and finally, people were listening to me."

Sheila didn't say anything, but I had a pretty good guess that she knew exactly what Rebecca meant. Finding a place to fit in was a very powerful magic.

"There were about ten of us," she continued. "Most were like me, college students. A couple were old school, like Caleb. We all wanted to do something, and Caleb had something more than protests and petitions." She shivered, even though the heat had finally started to kick in. "But that went too far tonight. He was so strong. He could always talk to us... you know." Rebecca tapped the side of her head. "And we were never cold. He said it was the warmth of our righteous cause. And when we were together, we could do... things. You saw. You saw what he did. People could have died. That's not what I want! I... I just want clean air and water." She started to tear up. "So when he told us to leave, I didn't go. I'd had enough. I couldn't." Rebecca looked out the window. The woods were dark, and there was hardly any light. "Where are we going?"

"Somewhere safe. Safer than here, anyway," Sheila said.

"You've seen what he can do. Do you think anywhere is safe?"

We were quiet after that. Mona's dream-catcher-and-claw combo swayed together like a pendulum, clacking against itself. It was the only sound for miles.

TWENTY-THREE

We made it back to the gas station without incident. No armies of raccoons and bears and birds tried to thwart us. For once.

Rett's camper was parked to the side of the one-story building. The main window was lit up, and I could see Mona, Rett, and Johnny inside, sitting around the front counter, laughing. They all looked relaxed, probably sharing stories about past eco battles. I pushed open the door and heard the tail end of their conversation.

"So there we both were"—Mona pointed at Rett—"covered in chicken blood. The campus security guards burst in the door. And we were caught. Red-handed."

Rett chuckled then elbowed Mona. "So then this one puts her hands out and goes, 'Brainsss...'" Rett demonstrated then doubled over, laughing.

Johnny laughed, too, a big, booming bark of a laugh, with his eyes closed. When he opened his eyes, he looked right at us, tapped Mona on the hand, and pointed to us.

Mona turned. "Well? Did you stop him?"

Sheila shook her head sadly. Mona frowned. Rett cursed softly and banged his fist on the counter.

"That asshole. I can't wait to shove—" Mona stopped mid rant when she noticed the half-naked girl hiding behind Sheila. She pointed at Rebecca and shouted, "Who the hell is that?"

Sheila put an arm behind Rebecca and nudged her forward. "This is Rebecca. Until recently, she was one of Caleb's followers, but they had a falling-out."

Johnny frowned. "And you brought her here? To my place?" His anger made him seem even bigger than his six-foot frame.

Rebecca paled, and if not for Sheila's firm hand at her back, she might have run out into the night.

Sheila held up a hand. "Hey, cool it. I said she *used* to be with him. She's not anymore. Caleb took all his protection off her and left her there half-naked. If we hadn't brought her, she'd have frozen to death."

Mona shook her head. "But, dear, if he was inside her head before, couldn't he still track her here?"

"Honestly," I said, "that might be the least of our problems."

Five minutes later, we'd filled them in on the details of the pulp mill implosion.

"Hold up," Rett said, clearly not willing to believe it. "He just... crushed an enormous pulp plant? Like literally crumpled it up like a piece of paper and dropped it on top of you?"

Sheila nodded grimly. "Yep. Just like that."

Rett's eyes were about to pop out of his head. "How did you survive?"

"It wasn't easy." Sheila knelt and scratched Orson's head. He was asleep on her foot. "But this little guy and I managed to shield ourselves. Took every ounce of our strength, though."

Orson woke up at her touch. *Yeah, don't mess with us! Now if you'll excuse me...* He dropped his head back on Sheila's feet and was snoring within seconds. She softly stroked his ear then stood back up. "Mona, we have to stop him. I have never seen power like this. The jerk who found that stone in Florida was an amateur, and when I was using it, I was trying to hold back. If Caleb has natural power like that, someone who knows magic and has no problem using it..." She left the thought hanging but it wasn't hard to finish it.

I turned to Rebecca, who had been silent. "Did you know he could do that? Was destroying the mill the plan?"

She shook her head. "No. We all just thought we were going to vandalize the mill. Make them shut down for a while." She shrugged. "I guess we did that." She looked at Mona. "And I'm very sorry about your cottage. It looked cute. But for some reason, Caleb was intent on either getting you to join us or taking you off the board entirely."

Mona squinted at Rebecca for a second then snapped her fingers. "That's it! I knew I recognized you!" She turned to Sheila and me, and I was very confused. "She was one of the ones who bailed me out when the Man arrested me at that town hall meeting."

Rebecca blushed faintly and had a small grin as she bent her head down to avoid Mona's gaze. "Yeah, that was us. Me and my boyfriend Terry. Well, ex-boyfriend now, I guess." She frowned. "Caleb was so excited for us to get to meet you. He couldn't stop talking about what an asset you'd be to us. How you'd been doing the real work for so long. How you'd shut down nuclear power, even! That impressed all of us. He was so upset when you didn't join."

Mona shrugged. "I'm not much of a joiner anymore. I've been disappointed by movements too often. It's either a bunch of dilettantes, or they take it way too far."

Rebecca sagged. "Yeah, well, you got us there. I got tired of the first group and wound up with the second. Now look at me." She glanced around the store. "On the run, on my own, without any friends. Oh yeah, and a pissed off Native American sorcerer after me."

Johnny Orono snorted. "He's about as native as Chief Wahoo. And an even bigger asshole."

Sheila looked puzzled.

"The Cleveland Indians' mascot," I whispered. "It's a buck-toothed cartoon."

Sheila frowned but nodded her understanding.

Rebecca was shocked. "What? He said that was the source of all his power! That because he was in tune with the great earth spirit Kisulk, he could do anything to defend her."

Johnny glowered at her, and Rebecca shrank backward, bumping into me. "That... *motherfucker!*" His eyes were angry enough to make me uneasy as well.

Rebecca was shaking. "I-I'm sorry! I had no idea!"

"Yeah, I bet you didn't, princess. I'm so tired of white people stealing our shit."

Rett put a hand on Johnny's shoulder. "Hey, come on. She's here to help us now." Rett looked up at Rebecca, who was still trembling and frightened. "Isn't that right, kid? You're gonna tell us all about Caleb and what he's up to, aren't you?"

Rebecca got herself together enough to very slightly move her head up and down.

Johnny glared at her. "Well then she'd better keep it up."

Rebecca gulped. She took a breath then seemed to remember that she was only wearing a dirty blanket. "Um, first, though... Anyone have a spare pair of sweatpants and a sweater?"

Johnny grumbled but stomped off to the back room. After a few seconds of audible grumbling, he emerged with a small stack of clothing. "This is from the clothing drive we just did. You can use the bathroom to get dressed." He pointed over his shoulder with his thumb. Rebecca took the clothes then meekly hurried away.

Once the door had clicked shut, Johnny spun and directed his anger at us. "Why did you bring her here? Are you trying to lead Caleb to us?"

Sheila stiffened but didn't wilt. She could be as soft and gentle as a starry summer night, but her backbone was steel. "I was not about to let a girl to freeze to death. From what I could read of her, she is sincere. She parted ways with Caleb."

Johnny wasn't impressed. "I don't buy it. We've done all we can to keep evil out of here, but she's going to bring him right to us. You said he can talk to his gang telepathically. How do you know he isn't following her now?"

I remembered how the animals had suddenly stopped chasing us when we got to the town line and crossed into Penobscot Nation territory. Apparently, Caleb had his limits.

Sheila scowled. "Then let him come. I'm tired of this. I'm tired of running through the woods and being chased by animals."

"Sheila," I said, "we just saw him destroy a factory without breaking a sweat. Can we really beat him?"

"No."

I turned. Rebecca stood behind us in faded jeans and a Patriots sweatshirt. I hadn't heard her come out of the bathroom.

"You won't be able to stop him. I'm sorry."

The room was quiet for a minute. Orson's wheezy snore was the only noise.

I spoke first. "Yes, we can. We've had to fight jackasses like him before. And they had big magic rocks and everything." I didn't mention what a struggle we'd had dealing with the previous jackass. That revelation seemed counterproductive.

She shook her head. "No, you don't get it. Maybe the lot of you can beat him. *Maybe.* But it'll be too late."

I glanced at Sheila then at Mona. "Too late for what?"

"I think he's going to destroy every power plant in the state. Maybe not even stop there. And I think he's going after the governor too. Just for fun."

TWENTY-FOUR

I was stunned. "What are you talking about? He wants to destroy every electrical plant in the state? Why? To what end?"

Rebecca stared at the floor as though it held all of life's secrets. "He wants to attack anything that has 'perverted nature.' So any polluter, any power plant—even hydropower, because it diverts rivers and affects the wildlife. And he wants to go after the governor that approved any of them as well. I didn't think he meant destroy. I just thought... well, I guess I didn't think it through."

"That's crazy." Sheila rolled her eyes then stared at Mona. "Yet, it sounds somehow familiar."

"Does wanting to leave a world for our ungrateful kids to inherit make us crazy?"

"Yes! If it means blowing up nuclear power plants, yes it does!"

Rett shrugged. "Well, he can't do that here. The only nuke plant in Maine shut down twenty years ago. All the spent fuel has been taken away. Still, if he can wreck enough power plants, he'll cause enough blackouts to start a panic."

Rebecca sighed. "I'm so sorry. Everything just sounded so... so right when he described it. Caleb would start by saying how we had to conserve and become energy independent. Who could argue with that? Then he'd say something about how we can no longer poison the earth. Sure! Then it would be the need to punish those who did. I thought he meant jail time, not murder. It would just keep inching up, a little at a time, until I was standing naked in a field and helping him harass an old woman."

Mona snorted. "I'm not that old, sweets."

Rebecca blushed.

"I know how it can be," Mona said. "It's easy to get wrapped up in a cause, and you can lose sight of things. I know I've done that. All I see is a forest, and I lose sight of the trees." She put her hand on Sheila's shoulder. "And the trees are important."

Sheila's lips curled up slightly. "Well, sometimes the trees could bend a little. Maybe not be so rigid."

Mona laughed. "I didn't teach you to be a weeping willow. Can't fault you for being an oak when you learned that from me."

Sheila grinned back. "Even an oak can sway a little, if the wind is strong enough."

"Like atomic winds." Mona cackled.

Giving me a puzzled look, Rebecca whispered, "What is going on?"

I grinned. "Just two old friends talking about forests."

Orson yawned and broke up the reconciliation. He stretched and shook himself awake then nudged his head against my leg. *C'mon. I need to go outside and pee on things.*

Of course he did. Perfect timing, as always. The first month we all lived together, he'd always seemed to have to go out and pee the second Sheila and I started to fool around. A big coincidence, no doubt.

I rolled my eyes and turned to the door. I jammed my hand in my coat pocket, looking for my gloves. An intense shock of burning cold greeted me. I yelped and pulled my hand out, dropping my glove on the floor. The two gummy-bear-sized figures skittered out. What with finding Rebecca in the aftermath of the pulp mill, I'd forgotten all about them.

Sheila rushed over to see what was wrong, and Orson sniffed at them.

"Hey, get away from those!" I yelled. "They're super cold!"

He whined but backed away.

Sheila glanced at my hand then crouched next to the carved crystals. "What are they? Where did you get them?"

"At the factory site. I found them after our fight with Caleb. They were on the ground, and it looked like they didn't belong there. I tried to pick them up and almost got frostbite. I've had them wrapped in my glove in my pocket since then, and they're still freezing cold."

Johnny came around the counter and gasped, his eyes wide. "Caleb had these?"

I shrugged. "I guess so. Him or one of his followers." I turned to Rebecca.

She nodded. "He had a bracelet. There were about a dozen of those on there, like little charms. He said they represented the souls of polluters he was out to take down."

Johnny turned pale then glowered with anger. "They're souls, all right. Trapped souls. Have you ever heard of the *chenoo*?"

I shook my head. None of us had. Even Mona was stumped.

"How about the wendigo?"

That I had heard of. "Isn't that kind of like a yeti?"

Johnny grimaced. "Kind of. It's a legend. A cannibal spirit that can possess people and turn them into monsters. Winters were a lot harsher a few hundred years ago, so of course, you can get stories about tribes turning to cannibalism when the supplies run out."

Orson pawed the door as the wind howled outside. *Really, so much nicer now.*

If Johnny heard him, he ignored the dog and went on. "The wendigo were pale giants, tall and emaciated, skin stretched over bones. They were ravenous, constantly needing to feed. In some stories, they're humans who become possessed because they're greedy. In others, they're mainly demons or monsters." He pointed at the little carved figures. "This is a little different. My auntie would... tell me stories about them." Johnny paused for a moment, maybe caught in a memory. "A chenoo is also an ice giant, ravenous and deadly, but these are always humans possessed. There are stories about women tricking the chenoo into sweat lodges, and once hot enough, they cough out their icy heart. A little figure of ice shaped like a man."

Sheila gasped. "That thing that Caleb turned into... Do you think?"

Johnny looked skeptical but gave a slight nod. "I've never heard legends about how people turn into those things, but it stands to reason. If you cough one of these up when you turn back into a human, I guess you could swallow one and become a chenoo."

I thought about the enormous muscled creature with the fused antlers and tight, stretched skin. At this point, magical Flintstones vitamins seemed as likely as anything.

Johnny went on. "The icy core was so cold, it burned at the touch. The hottest fire couldn't melt the ice. It was an indestructible evil. That's what Auntie always said."

Mona and Sheila glanced at each other.

"Do you think this could be another kind of those magic stones?" Sheila asked. "Like the purple one we found before?" She waved her hand, and the two little figures floated up in the air. She turned them carefully, inspecting them without touching.

Mona squinted at them. "It could be. I'd never heard about these stones until you told me about Florida. Still, it makes some sense. It could be why I feel so at home up here. Why the magic feels so strong."

Rett moved closer to the two women. "But where did he get them? Johnny's not selling chenoo souls next to the beef jerky out here."

Johnny started to say something then snapped his mouth shut and walked to the back of the store.

I turned to Rebecca. "Do you know anything about them? Where he found them?"

She shook her head. "He's always had that bracelet, at least since I've been with him."

One more puzzle to solve. How did Caleb go from being a regular old radical environmentalist and turn into a magical one? I thought about it for a bit, until Orson's whines interrupted me.

I hate to keep harping on this, but... He hopped from one leg to the other by the door.

"All right, pal. Hang on." I recovered my gloves, zipped up my coat, and took Orson out into the howling wind.

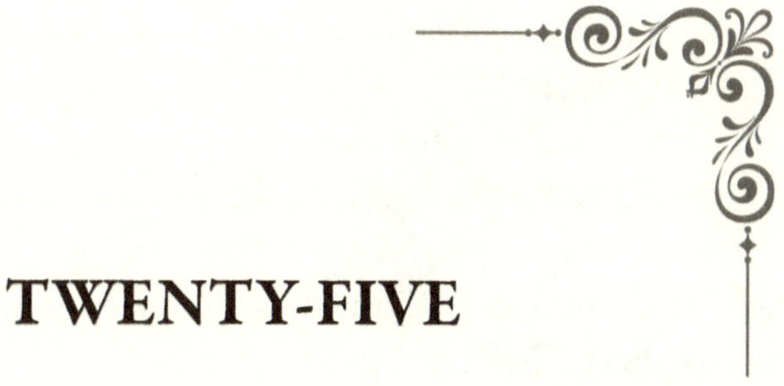

TWENTY-FIVE

Orson sniffed at broken sidewalks and piles of snow for a good long time. Very long. Quite frankly, a lot longer than someone who was desperate to pee would have taken.

"What is it, Orson?"

What? Just finding a good spot. There's a real art to it, you know.

"Stop it. I've seen you pee on a dead rat."

Had to let it know who was boss.

I grabbed his collar then squatted down to look him in the face. "What is it? You haven't been yourself all day."

He shook his head and yanked himself out of my hands. *Stop it! I'm fine!*

"What's going on? You and Sheila have been way too quiet since we got here."

He whined some more and pretended to sniff a nearby tree. *Scared.*

I felt the thought so softly, it took me a moment to make sure he'd actually meant it. "You're scared?"

He shook his head, making his little ears flop violently. Concerned as I was, it was hard not to grin. *No. She is.*

"Sheila? Why?"

Don't know.

"Is Caleb that bad?"

She won't say.

Sheila hadn't been herself for a few days, well before we knew who Caleb was. Maybe it was something else. "Is it Mona?"

Orson snorted. *Mom thinks she's a pain in the butt. Not scary. Scary annoying, maybe.*

"If it's not Mona, then what?"

Orson looked me in the eye. *She won't say. I don't know. Honest.*

Something was frightening her more than a crazy environmentalist who could turn into a horned ice monster and had tried to kill her a couple times. That wasn't good.

While I thought about that, Orson finished up his business and tugged on the leash in my hand. *Come on, let's go. It's too cold out.* He strained on the leash, nearly dragging me back to the store.

"Oh, *you're* cold now," I grumbled but allowed him to lead the way.

WHEN WE GOT BACK INSIDE, Mona and Sheila were still examining the little totem figures. Sheila rotated one slowly. Rett and Rebecca stood back a few feet while the two witches talked. I didn't see Johnny, so I guessed he was still in the back.

"What do you think?" Sheila asked.

Mona shook her head. "Never seen anything like it before. You know how hard that kind of transformative magic is. It's not something I can do."

I tried for levity. "Hey, Sheila turned me into a newt once."

They both stared at me like I'd just ripped a loud fart at Sunday mass.

Luckily, Orson had my back. *He got better.*

Sheila smiled and rolled her eyes. It might have been a grimace, but I was going to pretend it was a smile.

Mona went back to examining the charms. "I wonder... Are these one-time-use things? Can he reuse them? Could all of his little band take one and then he'd have an army of those things?"

Sheila shook her head slowly. "Your guess is as good as mine. This is the first I've heard of them. I don't see any markings on them. They seem pretty smooth and worn down."

Out of the corner of my eye, I saw Johnny come out of the back room. Sheila and Mona had their backs to him. I watched him discreetly as he stared at the two little figurines. His eyes were dark and scared.

I nudged Orson with my toe. "Stay here. See if Mom needs anything."

What's going on?

I tilted my head ever so slightly in Johnny's direction. "I think our host may know more about those things than he's letting on. Maybe a little alone time will help loosen him up."

Orson grunted and ambled over to Sheila. He plopped down and laid his head on her foot. I walked toward the back of the store, an aisle over from Johnny. I pretended to be fascinated by his selection of vintage canned meats until I was almost directly beside him. I looked over the top of the shelves. Johnny was still staring at Mona and Sheila. I cleared my throat, and he jumped a foot in the air. He recovered quickly enough to glare daggers at me before he landed.

"Hey, relax," I said. "You sure seem interested in those things."

Johnny grunted. I went on. "Weird, huh? How that Caleb guy suddenly turns up with these things? And how you somehow know so much about them." Johnny stared at me dangerously.

Most people probably wouldn't have pushed their luck with the bear of a man. "You know, it sure seems to me like you've seen those things before. And not just heard about them in a bedtime story. I'd really like to hear more about it."

Johnny seemed to deflate. His eyes darted over to the rest of the group, still looking at the figures.

I nodded toward the back door. "The ladies seem a little busy. I'm sure they don't need to hear all about my wild theories. Why don't we have a little chat, man to man? No need to get them involved."

With a grimace, he turned and walked to the back door. I followed after him. I stole a glance over my shoulder. Orson was still lying on Sheila's feet. He looked up at me as the door closed between us.

TWENTY-SIX

We walked out behind the store into a tiny lot. A sodium light over the door gave everything a yellow tint. A path led around to the dumpster on one side then out to the storefront. Trees behind us led into a denser forest.

Johnny wasn't thrilled to be talking to me, and he tried to regain some of his earlier bluster. "I don't know what it is you think you know—"

"Knock it off. I saw you in the store. The way you acted when you saw those little figure stones. That wasn't the first time you'd seen them."

Johnny shook his head. "I told you. My auntie told me about them."

"No. Your eyes were about to pop out of your head. I don't think that would've happened if you'd only heard about them. You probably tried to touch one."

He turned away from me, and I heard his muffled voice. "I did. Auntie wasn't looking, and I reached out to play with them. One of my friends had Legos, and these were the same size. I grabbed it and screamed." Johnny shivered. "I don't remember passing out, but I do remember waking up. Auntie was shaking me and shouting. When she saw I was okay, she cried in relief, and then she slapped me hard."

"So these belonged to your aunt—and now Caleb has them." I stared at him. "Wonder how that could've happened?"

Johnny spun on his heel and made a step to me. "You had better be extremely careful with what you say next."

"What? That your aunt taught Caleb all about magic? Come on, Johnny, someone had to teach him, and it wasn't Mona. He went from a protestor to an ecoterrorist to a telepath to a magician talking about native earth spirits. How many more native wizards are there out here? Seems obvious to me who told Caleb all about chenoos and Kisulk."

Johnny barked out a rueful laugh. "Of course a white boy would immediately jump to wrong conclusion." Johnny gave me a joyless grin, his skin looking jaundiced under the sodium security lights of the store. "Auntie didn't teach Caleb about magic."

Johnny snapped his fingers, and the security light popped out, plunging the small area behind the store into darkness. The only thing I could see was his golden glowing golden eyes. "I did."

I adjusted my balance, in case Johnny decided to do something stupid. I was pretty sure he was trying to scare me, but I needed to be ready if he tried to do more. Johnny was a big guy, but I'd fought plenty of bigger guys before, and I was still standing. Still, a big guy who could use magic was a little different.

I readied myself for a charge. But it never came. Instead, those two glowing dots disappeared, and I heard a deep sigh and a *whumf* as Johnny plopped down in the snow.

His voice was eerie in the darkness. "Do you know what it's like? To want something—I mean really want something so bad that your heart hurts—and be told you aren't good enough?"

"Is that what happened?" I asked. "You wanted to learn more magic, but she wouldn't teach you?" I heard a grunt of acknowledgement. "Did your auntie give Caleb the figurines that she smacked out of your hand?"

"No! She would never have given them to anyone. If she did, it would have been to me. But she said that they were too dangerous."

The lights popped back on as the door to the store flung open. Sheila and Mona burst through, hands raised and ready for action. And Orson was crouched low and growling.

I raised my hands to calm them down. "It's okay! We're just having a chat. No need to smite anyone."

Sheila pursed her lips in annoyance. "I swear, it's like you enjoy making me worry about you."

I let that one go. "Did you hear what he said?"

Sheila nodded without taking her eyes of Johnny. "Yes, for the most part. Once you stepped outside, Orson made us follow him to the back door. We heard all about him and Caleb."

Orson barked and growled at Johnny.

I walked up to him and scratched his wrinkly head. "It's okay, Orson. I'm fine."

Sheila and Mona turned their attention on Johnny. Mona sighed deeply. "Why didn't you tell us?"

Johnny hung his head. "Tell you what? That my aunt would rather train some random white boy than teach me her secrets? Yeah, I love to share that."

Sheila got right into his face and spoke very calmly. "Please, Johnny. We need to know. I'm sorry that it turned out this way, but people will die if we don't stop Caleb. You have to tell us everything that happened."

Johnny gave a small nod. He drew his knees up to his chest then leaned back against the wall. "About five years ago, I heard from some friends of mine in the Earth Liberation movement. They had a fugitive they were trying to hide, a real believer in the cause, but he'd gotten in some hot water and needed to lie low."

"Sounds like Caleb," Mona said. "Right after he blew up that fracking station."

Johnny shook his head. "I don't know anything about that. I didn't ask; they didn't tell me. Easier all around if things go sideways." He shifted on the ground. "So this Caleb guy shows up. Very committed, passionate, and charismatic. I take him into the woods and way off the beaten path."

"Out by your aunt, right?" I said.

"That's right. We hid him out there for a while and got to talking. He's so intense about the cause, so filled with righteous anger. He tells me how he's been doing everything he can to protect the earth, but it's not enough. Even if he were to blow up every fracker or oil well, they'd be rebuilt, and then it'd be right back to square one. He needed something to take it up a level."

Sheila was shocked. "So you decided to teach him magic?"

Mona slumped back into the wall not far from Johnny, her knees barely holding her up. Sheila went over to check on her.

She took a few shallow breaths. "I'm okay," she whispered then nodded to Johnny. "Go on."

"Yes, I told him about how he could become more in tune with the earth and use that power to help him in his work. I don't know a lot, but Caleb was eager to learn. I taught him how to listen to nature, how to summon animals. Small things. But that wasn't enough. When he'd mastered everything I could tell him, he begged me to introduce him to Aunt Johanna. She was our wise woman; she knew all the secrets of the earth. I had wanted to learn them myself, but she never taught me. She said I couldn't handle it all, said I didn't have the *resolve*. But she took one look at Caleb and what I'd tried to teach him, and she couldn't wait to tell him everything. She always wanted a disciple. Someone who would stick it to the people who'd destroyed our lands." Johnny went silent and stared off into the distance.

"Caleb was an eager student. Auntie was a demanding teacher. After a while, they both barely spoke to me. I came down here to run the store. I don't even think they noticed when I left. When I heard from Mona about the threats she was getting, I did what I could. I raised shields and wards to keep him out of here."

That must have been why the animals could only follow us as far as the town line.

He went on. "I haven't spoken to them in years, but when I saw those figurines, I knew what happened. I knew it was only a matter of time before Caleb learned everything and wanted more."

"What do you mean?" Sheila asked.

"Aunt Johanna would never have given those away. Not to anyone. If Caleb has them, there's only one way she would have let them go."

Mona groaned deeply and slid down the wall. Orson waddled over and rubbed his head on her knee.

Sheila sighed. "I'm sorry. But we need to go and check."

Johnny nodded. "Mona knows the way, but I'm not going with you. I haven't been back in years. She made her choices. I'm sorry if they came back to bite her, but I'm not going to clean it up."

Mona clucked her tongue sadly. "What happened, Johnny? We always looked up to you."

When Johnny didn't answer, I glanced at Sheila. We both knew about terrible families, and I could take a guess.

Johnny got up and slowly walked back into the store. We followed. Rett and Rebecca were still inside, staying warm by the counter. They started to talk as we approached, but Mona shook her head to silence them. In silence, we all left Johnny at the store, piled into the cars, and drove off into the night.

TWENTY-SEVEN

"**P**oor Johnny." Sheila sighed sympathetically as we bounced along in Mona's Samurai.

"I do know a little something about family letting you down. It always stings." I peered through the windshield. The headlights weren't doing much to pierce the blackness ahead of us. All I could see were the taillights of Rett's camper. Regular deer would be enough of a hazard, let alone Caleb-controlled ones.

Sheila turned away to stare out the passenger window. "How can the days be so short but feel so *long*?"

I yawned. "You're right about that. And it *has* been a long day. We've been going nonstop since Caleb showed up at Mona's last night." I hadn't had much sleep for about twenty-four hours. I'd gone longer than that before, but I'd been a younger man then. Much younger. And much more jacked up on energy drinks and caffeine. I rubbed my eyes and forced myself to stay alert.

I heard a *crack* next to me as Sheila rotated her neck. "That's for sure." She closed her eyes and was still for a second. "Mona tells me that Rett remembers a motel out this way. Maybe."

"I'm sure it has a great Fodor's rating."

I guess HBO and waffles are out of the question? Orson always had his priorities.

Sheila giggled then reached back to muss Orson's head. "Hey, who knows? Maybe there's a secret Disney resort out here! Hey, wake up!"

Oh! That was for me. I jerked my head up. Apparently, I was more tired than I'd thought. "Sorry! How much farther till we get there?"

Sheila paused. "Mona says half an hour or so. Are you going to make it?"

"I'll be fine..." I was getting so tired. All the adrenaline of the last day was ebbing out of me. I slapped myself and cracked open the window to let some freezing air buffet my face. Out of the corner of my eye, I saw a spark of something golden.

Suddenly, I was awake and alert, like someone had given me a Red Bull Frappuccino on an IV drip. My vision was sharper too. I could make out the edges of the road and the trees in much sharper clarity.

I tilted my head over to Sheila. "Thanks, babe."

She grinned. "Just a little shot of energy to keep us going, just channeling it through me and into you. I'd drive and let you nap, but I'm just as exhausted, and I can't drive a stick."

"How long will it last?"

Sheila shrugged. "It varies. Usually about an hour."

"And we're half an hour away?"

"Yeah, about that. Why?"

I arched an eyebrow and tried for a devastatingly sexy smile. "Because I'll have some time left over to put this energy to good use."

Sheila started to laugh. And laugh.

Orson woofed as well. *And people try to get* dogs *neutered.*

THE MOTEL WAS ABOUT what I'd expected—a small place, complete with fake-log-cabin décor that catered to summer tourists out to camp and hike through Maine. A long rectangle of identical rooms with the manager's office out front made it into an L. We took three adjacent rooms. Rett and Mona shared one, Rebecca took the next, and Sheila and I took the end. I made sure we were as far from Mona and Rett as we could be in case Mona had given Rett a little energy as well.

Our room was old-fashioned and a bit musty, with a flat brown carpet that probably hid only God knew what. The style was stuck in the seventies, but the room was clean, the bed was cozy, the heat worked, and the water in the shower was hot. That was enough for me.

Orson pounced on the bed. *There's HBO!*

We should all be so happy.

Sheila kicked off her shoes and curled up under the comforter. She was out in under a minute. I let Orson watch the violent delights on HBO until his even breathing told me he was resetting his loop for the day.

I turned off the TV and lay back on my pillow. I was still tingly from the jolt of magic Sheila had given me. Even though my body was spent and I could feel exhaustion creeping in at the edges, my mind was racing too much for me to drift off.

I sighed. I knew what we were going to find tomorrow. Johnny had said there was only one way Caleb could have gotten those trinkets from his aunt. I had a good guess as to what that one way was. I shivered.

My mind wandered back to our time in Florida. Orson and I had been looking for Sheila, and the trail led us to a run-down trailer park. I had wanted to talk to the woman who lived there, but our foes had beaten us to her. I had seen some terrible things in Iraq, but I wasn't sure I would ever forget what they did to that woman's body. Maybe Caleb had taken mercy on his teacher. Maybe he'd killed her quickly. But neither of those seemed like his style.

This wasn't helping me rest. I tried to focus on my breathing like Sheila had taught me. *Breathe in the good; breathe out the worries and fears. Whoosh. Whoosh. Whoosh.* It took a while, but I finally drifted off, centering myself on Orson's snoring.

I OPENED MY EYES AND saw a snow-covered field. Vast and endless, it stretched off to a distant tree line. The night sky was black and starless.

I shivered as the cold cut through to the bone. I had on sweatpants and a T-shirt. I tucked my hands into my armpits. The snow came up to my knees. I wiggled my toes and felt them touch ice and cold. I wasn't wearing socks.

I heard screams and wails. I turned my head to the right. Far off in the distance, I could see figures moving. I tried to run to them. I picked up one foot and tried to clear the snow, but I just sank farther into the drifts.

Across the field, I could see Sheila and Orson fighting the Caleb monster. The beast was effortlessly parrying whatever Sheila threw at it. The monster tipped its horned head back and bellowed at the sky, its bony jaw opening wide.

Orson lunged at Caleb and locked on to his ankle. With a kick, Caleb sent Orson sailing. Orson hit a thick tree trunk with a sickening crunch and a yelp. He fell into the snow, unmoving and silent. I opened my mouth to yell, but nothing would come out.

Sheila screamed. Bursts of blue light crackled from her hands and shot toward the creature. Caleb deflected the blasts away into the forest. Undaunted, she moved closer and closer, screaming and shouting, throwing more and more energy at him.

Then she got too close. Caleb reached out with his long ropy arm and grabbed Sheila by the throat. He lifted her up. Sheila gasped and tried to claw and kick at Caleb. He clenched his hand and cracked her neck. She went limp, and he dumped her into the snow.

A high-pitched keening whine came out of my mouth. I lurched forward, a step at a time, but kept falling deeper and deeper into the snow. It had gotten deeper around me. I tried to take another step, and I fell forward, burying myself in the snow. I opened my mouth, and snow filled it, suffocating me. I reached out desperately for something—anything—to grasp and pull myself out. My hand closed around nothing but icy coldness. So cold. My hand burned in pain. The cold and pain were making me shut down. Then everything went black.

I WOKE ON THE FLOOR of the motel, mouth open and buried in the cheap carpet. I felt hands on me. Someone was shaking me. As I came around, I realized Sheila was shaking my shoulders, saying something loudly that I couldn't quite make out. Orson was pulling on the leg of my sweatpants and whining.

As the fog of the nightmare cleared from my head, I could finally make out what Sheila was saying. "Wake up! Gabriel! Come on!"

My hand was still on fire, and when I lifted my head, I saw my hand was clamped tightly over my coat pocket holding the chenoo figures. The cold had seeped through the glove and the down lining.

Sheila and Orson let go as I sat up. I was covered in sweat, but Sheila leaned in and hugged me tight. Orson shoved his head under my free hand and rubbed himself against my side. He looked up at me with big, worried eyes.

"Oh, Gabe, thank goodness. You scared us both."

I was still catching my breath. "What... did you catch any of that?"

Sheila shook her head on my shoulder. "No, we heard you screaming and woke up to see you on the floor. What happened?"

"Nothing, just a stupid dream." I hugged her tightly and grabbed Orson as well.

I only dream about squirrels and hamburgers. Safer that way.

"Yeah, good advice, buddy."

I really hoped that it was just an anxiety dream and not a premonition caused by the magic boost Sheila had given me. I glanced at the coat pocket I'd been grabbing. Yeah, I definitely wanted it to be a stupid dream and nothing else.

TWENTY-EIGHT

I didn't get much sleep after that. I tossed and turned until I finally gave up at six in the morning. I showered, dressed, and went to check out the free breakfast the motel promised. The promise proved to be underwhelming.

I came back into the room with a plate of fresh-ish muffins and suspect-looking Danish. I balanced two Styrofoam cups of coffee as I pushed open the door.

Orson opened one eye and popped his head up. *Waffles?*

I shook my head. "Sorry. Got you a nice bran muffin, though."

He grunted in disgust and went back to snoring into the comforter.

Sheila stretched and sat up. "I smell coffee!" She smiled at me. "Any good?"

I shrugged. "I've had worse."

She giggled. "What an endorsement! They should put that on the side of the can."

Sheila sipped the lukewarm coffee and frowned. "You sure you've had worse?"

"Yep. I was in the army."

We sat for a minute, sipping coffee and nibbling the pastries. Aside from Orson, all was quiet.

Finally, I spoke up. "Are we ready to head out?"

"You don't sound very excited."

I grunted indifferently. "I have no interest in going out there and finding another dead person, and I'm ninety-nine percent sure that's what's waiting for us."

She took one more sip of coffee and gave up on the brown liquid. "You're probably right. But I have to know. And there may be some clue up there to stopping him."

"I know you're right. Doesn't make it any more fun, though." I took another sip of aggressively average coffee. "Mona sure acted weird when Johnny talked about him and his aunt teaching Caleb. How does she know her?"

Sheila shrugged. "She probably thought the same as you, that Johanna's probably dead, and that must've gotten her upset."

Orson rolled over and shook himself awake. *I changed my mind. Any Danish left?*

I tossed him a cherry one. He chomped down on it then scratched his ear.

After a few moments of chewing, I spoke up. "There's something else bothering me."

Sheila swallowed the last of her coffee. "What's that?"

"I still don't get why Caleb has such a hard-on to get your aunt Mona on his side. I get that she's magical. I get that she has some status in this hardcore environmental movement. But it's not like Caleb *needs* either of those things. He has followers of his own, and he can cause plenty of destruction by himself. So why?"

Sheila furrowed her brow. "It's been on my mind too. I've been too concerned with keeping us safe and stopping Caleb to think about it, but you're right. Why cause her so much grief that she needs to call us for backup? If he'd just gone about his business and destroyed power plants on his own without harassing Mona, we'd never have come up. Mona might even have cheered him on from the sidelines."

"I hope she's told us everything."

"Maybe," Sheila answered. "She does tend to conveniently leave things out."

Orson stopped eating for a second. *Her scones were pretty great. Maybe he wants those?*

Sheila grinned. "If only."

We had nothing to pack, so checking out was quick and, thankfully, uneventful. The morning air was crisp and cold, but the sun over the motel parking lot was beautiful. After a minute, Rett and Mona emerged from their room. They were holding hands tightly, as if they were clinging to a life raft. They were decidedly less chatty than they had been the day before, probably because they were worried about Johanna. Rebecca came out a minute later, shivering like she was still freezing from the previous day. She hugged herself as she trudged a few feet behind the others.

Sheila gave Mona a brief hug and nodded hello to Rett before they got into the car. Almost as an afterthought, Rebecca clambered in behind them, and they started off.

"How far are we going?" I asked.

Sheila pursed her lips. "Hard to say. Mona thinks it's only about thirty miles or so from here, but the roads aren't the best so..." She finished with a shrug.

Orson whined. *I don't suppose there's a McDonald's around here.*

Sheila couldn't help but grin. "Quiet, you. You've had enough McDonald's this week. Starting with mine."

Orson whined but licked her face. Sheila scrunched it up in mock disgust then gave him a hug. Orson flopped down on her lap. *I can't live on a little Danish! I'll starve.*

Sheila grunted. "You could stand a little starving. I'm losing feeling in my legs."

Orson snuffled. *Body shaming is bad.*

Sheila laughed and ruffled his head as we drove away.

AFTER AN HOUR OF HEAVILY rutted roads that wandered through the snowy countryside, we finally arrived at Johanna's residence. There wasn't much to see, just a row of three prefab mobile homes planted in the ground.

"This is it?" I asked. It barely qualified as a street, let alone a village. Not much sign of activity anywhere. No cars. No dogs running around. No TV noises from behind the doors.

Sheila nodded and pointed at Rett's camper. "Yeah, I guess so. They're getting out."

Orson rolled out of the Samurai and plopped into the snow. He thrashed to get his head up and sniffed around. *I don't smell anything.*

I looked at him, puzzled. "Yeah, I don't either. So?"

He practically rolled his eyes at me. *No, I don't smell anything. At all.*

I sniffed but didn't smell anything. That was no surprise, though. Sheila often told me that the jeans I'd been wearing for five days smelled terrible, but I never noticed anything. But then it hit me. The everyday smells of Maine—the pine trees and the crisp smell of the snow—were gone.

Sheila's eyes narrowed dangerously. "Someone's trying to hide something."

I grimaced, knowing right away what smell someone might want to hide.

Rett peered at the mobile homes. "Do you know which one is hers?"

Mona closed her eyes for a couple of seconds. Then she furrowed her brow. She snapped her head up, and her eyes popped open. "No. I can't tell." She strode over the Sheila. "Can you?"

I looked around the small motor court. There were no footprints in the snow, no pathways dug out. No one had been here in a while. I looked down at Orson, still snuffling the snow. "I bet you don't hear anything, either."

Mama was right. You are smart.

"Maybe they all went to Florida for winter."

Maybe we passed them on the way up. I could've waved. Or we could've stayed down there and waited. Orson shivered.

I put my hands on my hips. "Johnny didn't say which one?"

Mona shook her head. "I've never been to her house. We only met on the reservation."

The mistake was my own fault. I'd assumed the trail of destruction would make it obvious which trailer belonged to Johanna. Well, if something was blocking Mona, Orson, and Sheila from detecting Johanna, I would have to find her the old-fashioned way.

I trudged up to the door of the first trailer. The snow was hard and crunchy, but the crust didn't support my weight at all. With each step I took, the snow came up to my shin. It found its way up my pant leg and into my shoes. The steps of the tiny wooden porch out front were mounded with untouched snow. I carefully inched my way up, knocked on the door, and peered into the window. The curtains were drawn, but there was a gap in the middle to look through. No one was inside, the TV was off, and the threadbare couch was empty.

Following my lead, Rett took to the second trailer. He looked through the window and shook his head. "Nothing here."

We regrouped at the cars and stood staring at the third house. "Well," I said, "by process of elimination..."

We started up the path, spread out. We hadn't taken two steps when the door burst open. A mature native woman—thin with a hard, angular face—stepped out onto the porch. She stared at us and crossed her arms. "I've been expecting you."

Then the ground began to shake.

TWENTY-NINE

Apparently, Johnny had been wrong about Aunt Johanna. She'd obviously had no problem giving Caleb the chenoo stones, seeing as how we weren't standing over her dead body.

I had plenty of time to consider that as I flopped to the ground and rocked in the snow. Orson had a lower center of gravity and kept standing while growling his displeasure.

Johanna strode out to the top of the stairs. "Caleb told me you traitors would come." She paused a moment to spit at Rebecca. Even though she was a good twenty feet away from the porch, Rebecca flinched as though she'd been slapped.

Johanna turned her attention to Mona, who was still standing, although she was swaying back and forth. "And you're even worse. Turn your back on your allies when they need you the most."

Mona glared at her, and her back stiffened. "You aren't my ally. You never were."

Johanna scowled. "Really? I seem to recall things differently. I seem to recall a scared white lady who came scurrying to us when the feds were after her. I recall how, in return for sanctuary, you helped me teach my young friend all about how to use the secrets of nature to make his arguments more forcefully."

Young friend? Did that mean...

Sheila gasped next to me. "Mona! You didn't!" She glared at her aunt then nodded grimly. "Of course you did. No wonder Caleb's been after you. None of this 'join or die' garbage. You ditched him, and he wants payback."

Mona's eyes could have killed the lot of us. "You don't know anything about anything. Least of all this."

Johanna laughed mirthlessly. "That's right. And none of you are going to. It's time to end this." Johanna raised her hands to the sky and started to chant.

The ground I was sitting on rumbled. I struggled to get on my feet and had managed to get into a kneeling position when a shadow passed over my head.

I glanced up. A boxy little car was sailing toward Johanna's porch. She shrieked and dove out of the way as Mona's Samurai plowed into the side of her trailer. The cheap siding tore like paper, and the car landed in the front room. The shaking stopped as Johanna ducked and covered.

Sheila strode forward on my right, the air crackling with power and the tang of electricity. Orson waddled alongside, doing his best to keep up in the snow, but still growling a warning to anyone who messed with his mama.

"Yes," Sheila snarled. "Let's end this." She walked up to Johanna. Mona started after her, but Sheila spun on her heel and held up a hand to stop her in her tracks. "No. I am not dealing with you too. Once she's taken care of, you and I will have plenty to talk about."

Orson growled in agreement. Mona started to say something but for once thought better of it and backed away.

Johanna lay in the snow, moaning and bloodied. Sheila looked her over. "She got hit with some of the wood from the porch. She's bleeding, but it's not too bad. Rett?"

Rett was staring at her bug-eyed and didn't answer.

Sheila tried again. "Rett! Snap out of it!"

"Huh?"

"Do you have a first aid kit in your camper?"

Rett nodded but did not move.

"Well, go get it!"

Finally, he shook himself out of his stupor and jogged to the van.

I walked up to Sheila, very carefully. "Well, that was impressive! Although it's going to be very cramped in the camper on the ride back."

Sheila grimaced. "I didn't think about that. I just got tired of everyone here trying to threaten us."

"It's okay. I'm sure Mona's insurance will cover the tens of dollars that the Samurai is worth."

Orson whined *Good. I can't stand bouncing around in that thing. I miss the ragtop.*

Sheila relaxed enough to allow herself to smile.

Just then, Rett galumphed up with a tiny first aid kit and a roll of duct tape. "Here! I don't have a lot of bandages, but duct tape will work in a pinch." He passed the bundle over to Sheila. "I never go anywhere without duct tape! A thousand uses!"

She took the kit and started to tend to Johanna's head wound. "It's not that bad. Just looks messy." Sheila rolled Johanna on her side and swabbed at her head with some alcohol wipes, and that got her a sharp hiss. Johanna was coming around. Sheila tossed me the tape. "I don't need to deal with any more of her nonsense."

I nodded. I scooted over and quickly taped her wrists together behind her back. Like Rett had said, duct tape had a thousand uses.

Sheila murmured something under her breath. I saw her and Orson's eyes flash gold. Johanna's breathing softened and evened out. After a few minutes, Sheila had cleaned the wound and taped enough gauze to the side of Johanna's head that she didn't have to worry about the woman bleeding out.

Once that was done, she stood and marched over to Mona, who was trying hard to look nonchalant. "Now. We are going to get some answers."

"What do you mean? I have been nothing but honest with you."

"Are you serious? You forgot to tell us how you helped this nutter train Caleb? You remember him? The crazy guy who can turn into a giant monster and has tried to kill us a half dozen times. You didn't think that was an important little detail?"

"You think I'm working *with* them? Or trained them? What? I faked my house getting attacked?"

Sheila was seething. "I don't know. *Did* you?"

Mona was about to shout a reply when I slid between them, with my hands up to keep them apart. "Okay, easy! We can't afford to lose any more cars."

Both of them eased back a step.

"Now, Mona," I said. "From the beginning. That coffee shop wasn't the first time you met Caleb, was it?"

She shook her head. After a minute, she let out a deep sigh. "No. It wasn't." She nodded at Johanna, lying on the ground. "You heard her. When I first came out here, years and years ago, I was running from some trouble. Yes, Sheila, I know. 'What a shock.' Anyway, Johnny took me out here. It was remote and, as a bonus, on tribal land, which would keep the feds out of our hair. I spent a couple months out here and got to know Johanna really well, found out we were more than just kindred spirits. And she was well versed in her wise-woman traditions. We taught each other a lot of things."

"So when did Caleb show up?" Sheila asked.

"Like Johnny said—a couple years ago, probably right around the time he split from Rett. I got a message from Johanna. She had someone lying low out here who had turned into an A-plus student. He was really dedicated to the cause, and she wanted my help to teach him. And she didn't mean about the environment."

Rett spoke up. "You never told me. And Johnny never said anything."

Mona shook her head. "I hadn't seen you in ages, and Caleb only mentioned that you two had worked together, not that he'd blown up a fracking station and killed people. And Johnny had already left here because he was angry at Jo and jealous of Caleb. I didn't see a point in mentioning that I'd been helping his aunt. It'd only make him angry."

Rett got quiet and hung his head.

Mona went on. "All I knew was that he was passionate about the environment and was hiding out from the law, which could just as easily describe me. Johanna said he was gifted. He was a natural. Johnny got him started, then Johanna took off the training wheels. He picked up on things faster than anyone I've ever known except for..." She looked up at Sheila, who turned away from her gaze. "If I'd known he'd killed people, I wouldn't have helped!"

Rebecca spoke up. "Caleb leaves a lot of things out. I've noticed that."

Mona gave a curt nod. "He does. He also left out the little plan to blow up every power plant in the state." She looked down at the injured woman. "Johanna didn't say what the plan was. She just said it was something big and she was totally on board. She was going to do everything she could to help him. I guess that included the chenoo things." She sighed. "I can't say I was completely shocked. I hate the way people treat the planet. Add a layer of racism on top of it, it's hard to blame her for acting the way she did."

Sheila shook her head sadly. "What changed? You wouldn't have given it a second thought twenty years ago."

Mona sighed. "I know you think I'm reckless, but I really never wanted to hurt anyone. Honest. Even in Three Mile Island, I just wanted to scare people into stopping destructive behavior. Remember what I taught you? Every bad thing we do leaves a mark."

Sheila nodded. "I do remember. It's why I hold back. I don't want to hurt people if I can possibly avoid it."

Mona gave an embarrassed smile. "Wow, I taught you something worth remembering. So yeah, I fibbed a little. I didn't know if I could get you up here to help me if I just said, 'My student turned against me.'"

The thought formed in my head before I could stop it. *Just like Darth Vader!* This got me an eye roll from Sheila and a groan from Orson.

Dude, not the time.

I frowned. "Philistines, the lot of you."

Mona continued. "I needed you here, Sheila. You're the only one strong enough to stop him."

Sheila shut her eyes. "I could barely hold him off at the power plant, and I couldn't touch him when he was in that monster form. What am I supposed to do?"

Then I remembered. "Wait." I turned to Mona. "We were wondering why he cared so much about getting you on his side. If he was so strong, then he wouldn't have to worry about you. So why? Why send so much grief your way?"

Mona shrugged.

"You must know a way to stop him! Something he's scared of."

Mona protested. "But I don't! If I did, I would've used it when he came by my house."

"Maybe you don't have it, but you know something! Think. When you and Johanna were teaching him, did she mention anything? Anything at all?" While Mona searched her brain, I turned to Rebecca. "When you were with Caleb, did he ever say anything about that? Something that would have stopped him and his movement?"

Rebecca furrowed her brow. "I don't know. When he talked about anything that wasn't an 'action' like the pulp mill, he always spoke in generalities."

"Anything might help. We aren't sure what we're looking for."

Rebecca stared into the sky then closed her eyes. She frowned and shook her head. "I'm sorry, but all I can think of is that he's allergic to salmon."

Orson and I looked at her, dumbfounded. *What in the world?* Sheila and Rett shared our confusion.

But Mona reacted to this like she'd just shot down a triple espresso. "What? What did he say? Tell me exactly!"

Taken by surprise, Rebecca stammered out her answer. "Um, we were at a diner, getting breakfast. One of the guys was from New York, and he was complaining about how he couldn't get a good bagel out here. Caleb said it was just as well, since lox was the only thing that could hurt him. He laughed really hard at that. The rest of us kind of smiled, but I had no idea why that was so funny."

Mona almost whooped. "It's funny because he just told us how to beat him!"

Orson cocked his head and made a curious-sounding whine. *What? We're gonna hold him down and rub fish all over him?*

Mona laughed. "No! Lox doesn't mean smoked salmon! Lox is an evil spirit in the native mythology." That didn't help me any. After looking around at our blank faces, she continued. "Lox is the enemy of Kisulk. Remember?"

Sheila got it. "He said that the spirit of Kisulk flowed through him. So if he really is using that earth magic, then Lox is a way to fight him."

Mona nodded. "Right. Kisulk is like God. Lox is like the devil, roughly speaking."

Rett touched the crucifix around his throat. "So, to beat this guy, we are going to have to make a literal deal with the devil? I'm not so sure about that."

Mona shrugged. "Lox is less of a devil and more of an angry trickster wolverine."

Rett pursed his lips. "I don't know if that's reassuring. You're still talking about dealing with evil to defeat something. I don't know if the end justifies those means."

"Right, it's not like religion has ever been used to justify war or destruction or anything," Mona answered. "And you are taking this too literally. It's not an *actual* devil or wolverine. It's an idea that has power. He may think he's using the power of righteousness, but how noble is it if it's being used to kill people?"

I tried to steer us back on track. "But how does that help us? He's scared of this so-called evil spirit, then what? Can we summon it? Do I need to draw a pentagram or something?"

Mona grinned. "No, that's the good part. I know why he was so eager to recruit me. I already have what we need."

She almost giggled as she clambered into the shambles of Johanna's house. She went to her ruined Samurai, which had landed on the driver's side. She climbed on top and pulled open the passenger door. Then she lay down on her stomach, and her head and arms disappeared inside, her legs kicking in the air. A moment later she emerged, carrying something that looked like a dull, black claw. She jumped off the car, narrowly missing the door slamming down where her head just was, and ran back over to us.

She thrust her hand forward proudly. She held the dull black claw I remembered hanging from the rearview mirror of the Samurai. She smiled proudly. "I've had this in my car for years. I kept it for luck, but I almost forgot it was there."

Once when I was in LA, I went to the La Brea Tar Pits. In the gift shop, you could buy a souvenir saber-tooth tiger tooth. It was a resin copy of the fossils, about eight inches long. What Mona was brandishing looked a lot like that. I didn't see how that helped.

Mona nodded at the still unconscious Johanna. "It was a gift from her, years ago. When I first met her, she was so impressed with my tenacity. She called me the Badger." Sheila couldn't stop her smirk. "Yeah, yeah, I know. Anyway, she gave me a present. She said it was a badger claw." She went on. "The spirit of Lox is a wolverine, but in some translations, it's a badger. She said it was a connection to the past, to her ancestors. I knew from the moment I touched it that there was something to it, but I could never put my finger on what it was. You know, since I got it from her, not one speeding ticket!"

Orson chuffed. *The fact that car can't get over fifty-five has nothing to do with it.*

Sheila interrupted. "So this claw has somehow been blessed with the powers of Lox."

Mona nodded. "Johanna told me a story about how Lox had gotten into a fight with Glooscap—that's another hero of the folklore—and Glooscap had tricked him, and Lox got so mad, he punched a boulder in anger until his claw broke off. I guess that's supposed to be it."

Sheila looked at it. "And it's just been hanging off the rearview or rattling around in your glove box with the napkins and user manuals."

Mona shrugged. "You wondered why he was so interested in me. Johanna must have told him about the claw. Maybe he was so convinced that he had the spirit of Kisulk in him that he didn't want to take any chances. Anyway, it is magical. Go ahead, check it out."

She offered the claw to Sheila, who reached for it tentatively. She stroked it with the tip of her index finger and shivered. Orson shivered too.

"Whoa... You're right. There's something there." She looked at me. "It's like... like when I touched that stone in Florida. But different."

"How?" I asked.

"Well, that stone was pure power." She held up her hand with the ring that held the purple stone. "It felt electric, surging, like trying to block a water hose with your finger." She pointed at the claw. "This is powerful but... cold. It's not helping things flow. It's the opposite. It wants to drain them."

I nodded. "Then that's it. That's how we stop him. That claw might be able to stop Caleb if he Hulks out again."

Now we just have to find him. And fight him. And all of his followers. And scratch him with Mona's magic dream catcher.

I reached down to scratch Orson's head. "You're such a buzzkill. No treats for you. You're right, though. We need to find out where they're going to show up next."

Rebecca spoke up. "I think I know. Caleb said something before we went to the plant about how that was step one. He was going to create chaos, and then step two was going after those who didn't listen. Starting with the governor."

I thought back to the vision that Mona had shared with us. The portly man at the groundbreaking ceremony would be a great target for Caleb. First the pulp mill he'd approved, then the man himself. And what better way to lure him in than to destroy something he'd fought so hard to build?

"We need to get back to the mill," I said. "Right now."

Sheila nodded agreement. "You can bet he'll show up for photo ops and to check out the destruction of his mill. If Caleb's after the governor, that's the place to be."

Rett started back to the camper. "Let's get going. We can grab a paper on the way and make sure we're heading in the right direction, see if he had any comment on it. If he isn't there, we need to find out where he'll be."

Rebecca followed after him. Mona looked at the wreck of her car while Sheila beckoned me over to where Johanna lay.

"Help me get her inside." Sheila motioned me toward Johanna's head while she maneuvered her feet. With a grunt, we lifted her limp form and dragged Johanna into her home. It wasn't a lot better, what with the car-sized hole in the wall letting in the elements. But we got her into her bedroom, gently deposited her into the bed, and covered her up.

"How long will she be out?" I asked.

Sheila shrugged. "I'm not entirely sure. I was kind of pissed at her, so I may have been a little enthusiastic about it. Probably twelve hours, at least."

I nudged the bed frame with my foot. Johanna shook with the bed, but otherwise didn't move.

Orson whuffed. *Remind me not to get you pissed.*

Sheila laughed. "Try your worst, sweetie."

Mona was still in the living room. "I've had this car for ages. Got me through a ton of winters and bad weather." She gave us some side-eye. "Then you two come along..."

Sheila looked embarrassed. "Sorry."

Mona laughed and slapped her on the back. "Forget it. I'm gonna need more than just a car anyway. It may be time to try somewhere new. I hear Portland, Oregon, is nice. Less snow, anyway."

Sheila and Mona both sighed then looked around the ruin of the trailer.

"Just like when we tried to build a tree house. Right, Sheila?" Mona chuckled.

Sheila allowed a small grin then gestured with her head to Rett's camper. "Come on. Let's go stop a monster."

THIRTY

We all piled into the camper. Mona, Rett, and Rebecca rode up front in the cab, while Sheila, Orson, and I bounced around in the back, perched precariously around the card table.

Sheila held the claw and ran her eyes over it. "Quite the engagement trip, huh?"

I tried to smile. "I was getting tired of beaches."

Orson growled. *Speak for yourself. I get too much snow on my tummy.*

She put her hand on my knee. "I know. I'm lucky you're here."

I laced my hand in hers. "No, *I'm* lucky I'm here. If I hadn't met you, I'd be an angry and miserable person."

She leaned in against me, putting her forehead on my shoulder. I took the opportunity to stroke her long black hair. We sat like that for a few minutes as the camper's tires bounced beneath us. I reached over with my free hand to take hers, and I noticed she had the purple ring on. The stone was dull, but I knew it would flare up when needed.

"You're still wearing it."

She nodded. "I haven't taken it off since the mill." She took a deep breath. "You and Orson were right about that. I have to be ready. I can't let anything hold me back if he comes at us again." She closed her eyes and exhaled through her nose. "It's like holding on to a joy buzzer, just a constant tingle. I'm getting used to it."

I squeezed her hand gently. Maybe it was the power of suggestion, but I swore the ring gave off a dull thrum.

She stared into my eyes, hard. "I was holding back. I was scared to lose control. But I'm more scared to lose you." She leaned into me and kissed me deep.

I held on to her for dear life. After a few seconds, I felt something bump into my leg.

Hey, what about me?

Sheila leaned over and picked up Orson. She grunted as she lifted him up to sit on her lap. "That goes double for you." Orson shifted his chubby little body, causing Sheila to wheeze. "You need to lay off the junk food." She glared at me. "You give him too many treats."

I shrugged. "I'm just trying to buy his love."

Orson gave her a big sloppy lick. *Yup. And it's working.*

Sheila rolled her eyes and wiped off her face. Then she giggled and grinned, rubbing her nose on Orson's.

Sheila would do anything for us. So would I. Well, I didn't know how much good I could do against a shape-shifting ecowarrior, but I would do everything I could.

AFTER ABOUT TWO HOURS of bouncing down back roads, Rett stopped to gas up the camper. I went into the gas station and snagged a local paper. The destruction of the mill was the front-page story in the *Bangor Daily News*, and there was a sidebar article about the governor coming up to the area to survey the damage and promising to rebuild as soon as possible, plus some strong language about dealing with those responsible.

Yeah, good luck with that.

We were on the right track, at least. Once the truck's tank was full, we would head back on our way. I took a minute to stretch out after rocking around in the camper. Another hour to go on the road, then hopefully, we would get there before Caleb caused any more destruction. The paper said the governor was giving a press conference at three in the afternoon, so that gave us a little time to meet him before things got even more out of hand. If Mona's memories were anything to go on, Caleb would want to milk the moment for all it was worth. He would likely show up in the loincloth-and-antlers getup, make some dramatic pronouncements, then attack the governor in front of the cameras. That had to guarantee publicity.

The gas station sold maps, and they had a *Maine Atlas & Gazetteer* up front by the magazines. I bought a copy and flipped to the page for Caribou as I went outside.

Mona and Sheila had also gotten out to stretch and were leaning against the side of the camper as I walked up. Sheila noticed me studying the map.

"Looking for a short cut?" Mona asked. "I know the camper's not that great to ride around in, but I don't think it'll make much of a difference."

I grinned. "Not quite. I was thinking about Caleb. We know, based on our own experiences, that he's pretty theatrical, right?"

Mona rolled her eyes. "Yeah, that's the polite way to put it. More polite than 'psycho drama queen,' anyway."

I held up the newspaper. "The press conference starts at three. I'd lay even odds that Caleb's not going to make a move until it's well underway and all the cameras are rolling."

Mona looked unimpressed. "Yeah, sure. That gives us a little more time, but how does it help?"

"Well, as powerful as he seems, I'm pretty sure he just can't materialize out of thin air." I looked from Mona to Sheila. "Right?"

Mona snorted. "Of course not! Don't be ridiculous."

"A couple years ago, I thought talking dogs were ridiculous." Orson whined in disapproval, and I bent down to scratch his head. "I know better now."

Sheila helped out. "Our... skills don't work like that. It's more about channeling the forces around us and manipulating them. No one can create something out of nothing. I'm pretty sure, anyway." Pretty sure was as good as we were going to get.

I pointed to the map of Caribou in the *Gazetteer*. "Get Rebecca out here. I have an idea, but I want her to confirm a few things."

Mona banged on the door of the pickup, and Rebecca's head popped up in the passenger window. She blinked a couple times. Apparently, she'd been trying to nap. She cranked down the window and leaned her head out. "What is it?"

"When you guys attacked the mill yesterday, where did you come from?" I asked.

She closed her eyes. "There was a hill beside the parking lot. Behind it there was a field that led up to the edge of the forest. Caleb gathered us in the field by the forest."

I looked at the map. I saw the little dashed lines indicating the topography of the hill and the ribbon of white before a mass of green. That would be a good spot to sneak in from the forest, make a dramatic entrance over the hill, then melt away into the woods again.

I pointed at the map. "If we can stop them there, then we'll keep the risk of injuries to a minimum."

Sheila grimaced. "You mean injuries to *other* people. Ones who aren't fighting him directly."

"Well, yeah. Not much help for us though."

Sheila shook her head softly. "I really miss the simple joys of fighting jilted lovers in a Bible park right about now."

"I promise to get us a season pass when we get back to Orlando."

Sheila smiled, and her eyes crinkled adorably.

Rett finished pumping the gas and hopped back into the cab. "Come on. We'd better get going."

I sighed. "Let's go." I held the door open for Sheila, and she hauled herself back into the camper.

I held the door for Orson, but he whined again. *Tell me you got me some jerky treats... High protein... Low carb...*

I winked at him.

He gave me a big smile then scrabbled into the back.

THIRTY-ONE

At one o'clock, the road from Caribou to the ruins of the mill was clogged with traffic. Some black SUVs, probably carrying the governor and his security team, tried to slip past the news trucks that were plodding along and looking to get set up for the live press conference.

We drove past the turnoff and stayed on the main road. There was almost no traffic on this side, since all the press were coming from Caribou and other points to the south. About a half a mile past the turnoff, Rett coasted to a stop on the shoulder. He turned on the hazard lights then jumped out to put up orange safety triangles. Anyone driving by would assume we had broken down and gone for help.

We gathered on the side of the camper away from the road. I examined the map book and tried to gauge where we were relative to the plant and where we thought Caleb would pop up.

"It looks like we stopped just before that curve up ahead." I pointed at the map then to just ahead of the camper. "So, if we go in... there"—I indicated a gap in the trees across the from us—"then we only have to go about a quarter mile to that field where Caleb is getting ready."

Orson peeked around the side of the truck and grunted. *It looks like there's two feet of snow in there! How am I gonna walk through that?*

Sheila nodded at me. "Gabe will carry you if he needs to."

Orson slobbered on my feet in thanks.

"Why me?" I asked.

Sheila cracked her knuckles. "I need my hands free to cast. Besides, you keep giving him fatty treats. You can carry him around for a bit and think about that."

I sighed. "Fair's fair. I hope you can make it through the snowdrifts, pal, or no more burgers for you."

Orson whined. *Aw, come on. I'll think light thoughts.*

I scratched him behind the ears.

As we headed across the road, I examined the gap in the trees. No footprints. The snow was fresh. And no sounds, either. The woods were quiet. Even the traffic noise from the press convoy faded into silence.

I glanced at Sheila and Mona. "You sense anything?"

Mona frowned. "You mean like a big flashing sign that says Trap Ahead? No, I don't see anything like that."

Sheila agreed. "I don't get any feelings from this. Either he isn't expecting anyone to come this way, or he doesn't think we're important enough to worry about."

Orson growled. *Well, we'll show him!* He bounced forward and leapt into the opening, and the snowbank promptly swallowed him up. The drift was deeper than it looked, and as he thrashed about, only his hindquarters were visible.

It was all Sheila and I could do not to laugh as we fished him out.

"Stop squirming." Sheila giggled.

Stop laughing! I was trying to be heroic.

"Okay, okay," I said, trying to calm him as I hoisted him out. "You can still be heroic while I carry you." I grunted as I shifted his weight. "Oof, Mama's right. You really do need to cut down on the treats."

Orson growled his displeasure.

One by one, we waded into the forest. The drifts were deep, and keeping upright was a struggle. Rebecca shivered and tried to keep her balance. Mona and Rett leaned on each other for support and balance. The snow was powdery and offered little support. With each step, it went up to my knee.

Sheila lurched forward and steadied herself on my shoulder. "Well, Caleb certainly didn't come this way. How much farther do you think it is?"

I checked my watch. It was 1:20 p.m. We'd been schlepping for ten minutes. "I hope not much longer. I swear Orson got heavier since we started."

Just more of me to love.

I sighed, and it was at that moment that Orson chose to fart at me. "Damn dog!"

What? I'm sure I'm lighter now.

Sheila smacked us both. "Knock it off. We can't let him know we're here."

Yes, Mom. We both thought it at the same time. Sheila gave us a quick frown then trudged ahead. The woods were quiet—and too cold for any birds to be chirping. No rustling of woodland creatures. Just our breaths and the crunch of the snow under our feet.

Finally, we came to the clearing. There was a hill to our left, with the ruins of the plant on the other side. I looked around but didn't see Caleb or his crew anywhere. The field looked very familiar. I had no idea why, probably because pine trees all looked alike after a while.

Maybe they stopped at the gas station to get changed. Orson squirmed in my arms. The snow wasn't as deep here, so I put him down. He shook himself and started to sniff around.

The rest of our party had made it to the edge of the woods. Mona and Sheila looked about. "Did we miss them?" Sheila asked. "Should we go up the hill after them?"

As I was about to agree with her, Orson gave a low growl. *No, we didn't miss them.*

I looked over to see what he was growling at. From the woods across the field, our old pals came out in their loincloths and antlers. Caleb strode to the front of the pack and called out, his voice enhanced to boom through the air and inside our heads.

"About time. I was sure you'd be back. Now, hurry up and get killed so I can continue with my mission."

Mona snarled at them. "Time to show you what a real witch can do." The air around her crackled and shimmered. She wildly flung her hands at Caleb, causing bursts of snow and dirt to leap up around him.

He shielded his face then screamed at his followers. "What are you waiting for? Get them!"

They started to run at us. Mona sprinted across the tree line to meet them.

"Mona!" Sheila called after her to slow her down, but she wasn't having it. "Come on!" The familiar purple tinge filled Sheila's eyes. The air around her crackled as she followed Mona, Rett and Rebecca on her heels.

Orson started to lope over. He looked back at me. *What are you waiting for?*

What *was* I waiting for? I took a step, then I remembered where I had seen the field before. The dream where Sheila died.

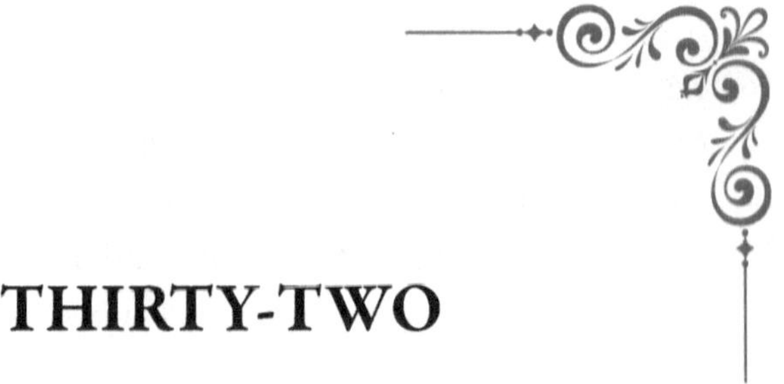

THIRTY-TWO

Orson barked, and that was enough to snap me out of my thoughts. If this was my nightmare coming true, it wasn't going to happen because I stood around like a coward.

Mona was screaming profanities at Caleb, sparks at her fingertips. I could sense Caleb's smirk from where I stood. He gestured, and his horde of misguided idealists advanced. I counted ten of them running to meet us.

It was my turn to smile. I may not have known much about magic, but I sure could smack a guy really hard. That was something I could help with. I shouted to Sheila, "You handle Caleb. We can deal with these assholes."

I know, sweetie. Take care of yourself. She nodded and turned to join Mona.

Orson bounded up next to me. *Don't you hog all the fun.*

"Wouldn't dream of it."

After a few steps, we met the first two brave souls. One was young, not long out of college, and the other was a grizzled vet of the movement. The old guy carried a club that looked like a heavy tree branch. He raised it overhead to swing down at me, but he was too slow. I stepped inside his reach and blocked his arm with my left then gave a tight uppercut with my right. I heard his teeth rattle as his jaws slammed together. Then his eyes lost focus, and he went down.

Joe College was a step behind, and he stopped when he saw how I laid out his pal. Orson took the opportunity to jump up at his midsection and knock him down. He landed on his back, then Orson landed on his stomach. The guy wheezed, the breath knocked out of him.

Orson growled, snapped at him, then sniffed the air. I heard his warning a second too late. *Behind you!*

I spun just in time to see another of Caleb's goons get his cheek deformed by a monk with brass knuckles. As the guy collapsed to the snow, Rett shook out his hand. "I'd prefer a hockey stick, but those are hard to hide in the robe. These babies, though..." He wiggled his hand for emphasis.

I nodded and pulled my leather slap stick out of my coat pocket. The weapon was one of the only things I'd kept from my time in the Army. "I like my blackjack, but those are pretty nice."

If you two could stop comparing your toys... Orson growled.

I looked up. Two men and two women were coming toward us.

Rett grinned. "Shall we?"

Whatever Caleb had given his team in terms of magic hadn't translated to hand-to-hand combat. Hopefully, they made up for it in enthusiasm. The two men were both college aged as well. They were pretty big, but I doubted they'd ever even been in a bar fight. *Tough for them.*

One came up to me and threw a wild haymaker, which I ducked easily, then I smacked his knee with my blackjack as he went past me. He screamed and collapsed, grabbing his knee. If he was lucky, it was a bad sprain. If he wasn't, he would have eight weeks of bed rest to think about what he'd done.

Rett obviously had years of experience as a brawler and fighting dirty. He got low and slugged a guy in the gut then hit him again slightly lower. The youngster's eyes crossed, and he sank to the ground.

I heard a woman scream, and I spun to the right. Orson had clamped down on the ankle of a young woman, who was desperately trying to shake him off. She fell on her back in the snow.

Only one more follower was left standing—a middle-aged woman who stood her ground as Rett and I turned to face her. "How dare you?

How dare you interfere when we are trying to save our life-giving mother!" Her eyes had a familiar purple tinge.

Welp. I guess Caleb taught at least one of his followers a couple party tricks.

"I'll teach you to meddle in things you can't possibly—" She stopped abruptly and fell face-first into the snow. She'd been rudely interrupted by a tree branch to the head.

Rebecca stood over the woman's body, holding the club. "Oh, shut *up!*" She glanced in our direction. "You have no idea how long I've wanted to do that. She couldn't keep quiet for ten damn seconds. Life-giving mother..."

Seven down. That left three more. I scanned the field and saw three more bodies lying motionless in the snow. I guessed a few of them had tried to keep Mona and Sheila from Caleb. Big mistake.

Across the field, Caleb was fending off our two witches. Mona screamed and flung her power at him. Sheila looked calmer, but I knew her fury was just as intense. The energy around them was like a haze on a summer day. Caleb was holding his own, blocking and parrying what they were throwing at him, but frustration was starting to set in. Anger creased his brow. Mona and Sheila hadn't broken a sweat.

"Give it up!" Mona shouted. "You're done. You aren't going to hurt anyone else today." She punctuated that with a burst of purple sparks that rained down on Caleb.

He sneered angrily. "No. I am never done. I will never be done as long as Kisulk speaks through me."

"Oh, enough with that bullshit." Mona cursed. She and Sheila both cast at the same time. A shimmering wave of gold crossed the distance between them and knocked Caleb on his back.

He glared daggers. "I'll show you what's bullshit. Kisulk is my strength. And your undoing."

He brought his hand to his mouth. Too late, I realized what he was doing—swallowing one of the chenoo stones.

Caleb flinched and curled his body up on the ground. Then the change began. His arms and legs lengthened and were covered in ropy muscle. Bones cracked and grew. His skin became a pale gray hide. And the antlers he wore fused to his skull, growing into a bony crest.

He stood, unfolding himself to eight feet. He rolled and cracked his shoulders, each hideous pop of bone resembling an awful laugh.

I looked across the snowy field. Horned, muscled, and bony, Caleb towered over Sheila and tipped his head back to howl. Orson barked and ran to protect his mama. He growled and snapped at the creature.

I started to run as best I could. I cut across the meadow, but the snow was deeper than I'd thought, much deeper than at the edge of the forest where we'd been fighting. As I waded through it, I was sinking in up to my shins with every step. *Shit.*

Caleb swung a clawed hand at Sheila. She leapt back. Her eyes flashed dangerously, and purple sparks flew from her hand as she swung her fist in a wide arc at him. The magical blow connected and rocked his head. Caleb shook it off and stepped toward her. Even from this far back, I could see the eye sockets in the skull glowing in the blackness.

Mona shrieked and ran to protect her niece. The girl that Orson had been biting and the guy Orson had jumped on tried to run to help Caleb, but Rett and Rebecca intercepted them and started to fight them off. That just left me. I tromped as fast as I could.

It wasn't fast enough. The snow seemed to be devouring me, like quicksand in an old cartoon. I could barely move, only watch in horror.

Caleb bounded forward. The snow wasn't stopping him. Two bounds, and he was in front of Sheila. Mona slid in beside her and tried to slice at him with the claw. Caleb backhanded Mona, sending her flying into a snowdrift. He casually picked up the claw then turned back to Sheila. She threw her hands up, trying to create a shield, but Caleb raked the claw downward. Sparks flew at the impact and sent her flying backward. Sheila struck against a pine tree and slumped down into a heap.

Mama! I could hear Orson's wail of anguish across the field. He howled and tried to get close to protect her, but he was handling the snow about as well as I was. He flopped over and tried to get between her and Caleb. The monster advanced, letting out a low guttural chuckle.

I lurched forward but tripped and fell forward into the snow. I tried to brace myself in the snow but wound up facedown in the drift. I slipped and was struggling to get up when I saw something in the snow. The chenoo stones. My eyes widened. They must have fallen out of my pocket.

Orson barked and growled, doing his best to ward off the monster. He backed up toward Sheila, who still hadn't moved. Caleb advanced slowly, relishing his moment. He wouldn't wait much longer.

If Caleb had swallowed one of those things to become that, then I knew what I had to do. Sheila would tell me it was stupid, that I didn't know what would happen, if it would even work, or if I could change back. I might burn a damn hole in my throat or stomach and just plain die. All of those were very good points. Very sound and logical. And I was going to ignore them all because I didn't have any other choice.

I clambered to my feet and struggled on. Only a few more feet. Caleb reared back and started to swing his gnarled and clawed hand at Orson. That was it. If I was going to do it, I had to act now.

"Hey, asshole! You with the ugly, fucked-up antlers!" I wasn't great at witty banter under pressure. It was enough to get Caleb to turn my way. *Great.* "I have had enough of your shit." I snatched the figurine from the snow. The cold made my hand clench hard around it.

I felt Orson in my head. *What are you... You can't be thinking...*

Yeah, pal, I am. Before I could change my mind, I shoved the chenoo stone into my mouth and swallowed it.

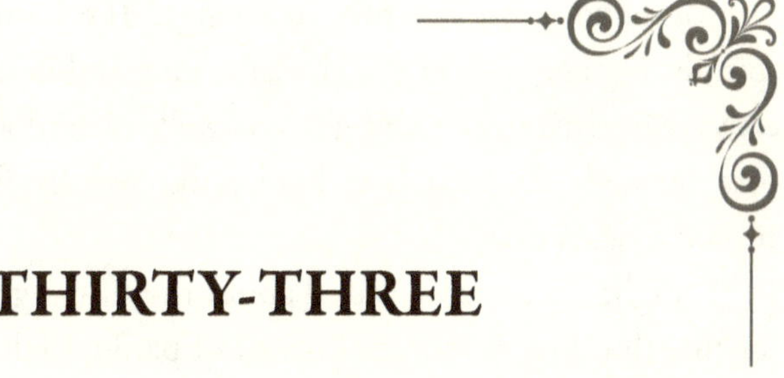

THIRTY-THREE

The pain was hot. Searing. I felt nothing but pain as the stone inched down my throat, burning every fraction it advanced. I dropped to my knees. When the stone reached my stomach, the pain bent me over on all fours. My vision narrowed, going darker. Everything was streaked, smeared like a time-lapse photo. I gasped, but the air wouldn't come.

Shit. This was a terrible idea.

Maybe someone magical like Sheila could handle it. Caleb, apparently, could. Maybe even Orson. I wasn't magical. I was just desperate to stop a crazed madman from hurting the woman I loved. I had been told that love was a powerful magic. Not powerful enough, though, it seemed.

The pain hit my stomach like a roundhouse kick, forcing me to the ground. I curled into a tight ball, my whole body shaking. Through the tears, I could see the fuzzy shape of Caleb coming toward me. The ringing in my ears couldn't mask his cruel laughter.

The last thing I saw before my eyes shut tight was a skull topped with antlers at the end of a tunnel of light. Then blackness swallowed me. Then silence.

The cold pain spread throughout my body. It flowed through my blood like a river of ice water washing away fear and doubt. My body unclenched. My spine stiffened. My fingers had just before been digging welts into my palms, but now they stretched out straight.

My hands were the first to change. The joints became bony and spindly. My chewed-up nails became long and tapered into razor-sharp claws. My arms jerked and grew as well. I heard a rip as my shoulders tore through my coat. My bare arms, usually fish-belly white, had turned a sickly gray.

I might have been worried about these changes if it weren't for the icy tide flooding my brain. Instead of panic, I felt cold and hard. Like my new muscles. Like my claws. Like my heart. Like the heart I was going to tear out of Caleb and eat in front of him.

I blinked. The pinpricks of light and tunnel vision were gone. The ringing in my ears was gone. Everything was clear. I could count pine needles on the trees across clearing. But all I saw was Caleb. He stopped, no longer laughing.

I stood, rolled my shoulders, and flexed my back. Shreds of cloth fell to the snow around me. I felt the wind and the snow, but the cold fed me. I could feel two nubs form on my head. They burst through the skin, sharp and pointed. Feeling the horns, I smiled. I had never felt such strength and power.

Today you die, Caleb.

I leapt up to my feet and tipped my head back. I wanted to roar, so I did. I felt everyone's eyes on me, and I tasted their fear. It was delicious.

Caleb charged at me. I bounded to meet him. We crashed in midair. I raked my claws over his back. He howled. I could feel the sparkle in my eyes. *Good. Now you get a taste.*

We fell to the ground, wrestling and clawing. I couldn't get a good punch in, but he couldn't, either. We rolled in the snow, and I wound up on top. I raised my fist to drive his head into the earth, but he kicked up, sending me sailing. Primal instinct kicked in. I flipped in the air and landed in a crouch.

I smirked. *Is that all you got?*

He charged again. I leapt, but this time, he ducked low and raked my exposed stomach. I fell hard and clutched at the scratches. The blood oozing out looked black. He laughed, and my fury surged. I rolled onto all fours and scrambled forward, catching him around the waist. I felt my horns gouge his flesh. I drove him to the ground and pummeled his face. His bone mask cracked under my fist. I cackled and hit harder. A few more punches, and his bone plate would be shattered. *This is so easy.*

Then a sharp stab of pain struck my side. I glanced down to find a black claw in my flank. Caleb's cracked face smiled up at me. I'd seen him take the claw from Mona, but I'd been too jacked up on the power rush to think about it.

I slid off him and into the snow. The cold fire was seeping away. Now it was just cold. Caleb stumbled to his feet and lurched forward to kick me. He lifted me off the ground and a few feet away. The claw fell into a snowdrift, staining the snow black. The pain lessened, but it was still enough to keep me down.

The claw lay between us. Caleb staggered, but he was strong enough to walk toward me and leisurely finish me. I tried to roll up to a sitting position, but my new body was having none of it. I flopped on my back and tried to lever myself up with my elbows.

Caleb took one more step toward the claw. Then a buffalo attacked him.

No, not a buffalo. Something at least as big as a buffalo smashed into him, knocking him over. This thing had claws and teeth and growled. *A bear? No...*

Then I heard Orson in my head. *Can't let you hog all the fun.*

Barely recognizable, Orson stood over the fallen beast and howled. His stout little body had blown up to as big as a grizzly. His brown-and-white coat had turned gray and black. His underbite was comically large, showing two rows of sharp teeth that were snapping at Caleb. He was frantically trying to block the bites with his forearms, so Orson chomped down on his arm.

I looked back at the shreds of my coat. The pocket where the stones had been was torn open. *Stupid dog.*

Who you calling stupid?

I checked my side. The blood had slowed to a trickle. My new freak body healed pretty quickly.

I heard a yelp. Caleb had kicked Orson off him, and he flipped in the air. Orson landed on his feet with a growl. I lumbered to my feet. Caleb had recovered enough to stand. For a tense moment, we all stared at each other from different points on a triangle. Then with shouts and howls, we all charged toward the center.

Orson went for the legs. I went for the head. I caught Caleb in the chest, and he pounded my back. Orson tore into Caleb's ropy calf and didn't let go. Caleb tried to kick at Orson, but I was keeping him too busy for him to aim.

I heard noises around me, but I had no idea what was going on. My whole world was the small circle where Orson and I were fighting Caleb. We tumbled in the snow. Caleb landed a kidney punch where he'd stabbed me before, and the pain shot through me. He kicked Orson hard enough to dislodge him and make him shriek. I found a good-sized rock near where I'd fallen and flung it at Caleb's head. It connected hard and drove him to the ground.

We all staggered to our feet. Again. As long as the magic kept healing us, there would be no end to this.

Unless...

I touched my side where Caleb had stabbed me. I scanned the ground and saw the black blood spattered on the snow. Next to it was the claw.

Orson saw where I was looking and grunted. Then he charged Caleb again. Caleb saw me take off toward the claw. He took a step to block me, but by then, he had to deal with an angry ball of Orson scratching at him. He tried to shove the giant dog out of his way, but it was too late. I dove for the claw and grabbed it.

It was heavier than it looked, but it balanced in my hand like it was made just for me. I sliced through the air and crooked a finger at Caleb, urging him to come at me. Caleb lunged at me, enraged. Orson jumped on his back and knocked him down. I grabbed the claw with both hands and plunged it toward Caleb's head.

It raked down the side of his bone plating. It left a furrow, but it didn't seem to affect him much. He growled and swatted at me. I was knocked back, the claw falling to my side. We both dove for it. Orson jumped at Caleb, but Caleb rolled, grabbing Orson by the scruff, and got him into a headlock. Orson squirmed and snapped, but Caleb had a firm grip. He worked his hand in between Orson's jaws and pulled.

Orson writhed and scratched at Caleb's arms. His claws made a mark in the muscle-wrapped bone, but not enough to get him to let go. I picked up the blade. I tried to tell him to let Orson go, but my intended words came out as a howling gurgle. He replied with a low cackle and flexed harder, slowly pulling Orson's jaw apart. He yelped in pain.

"Let him go!"

Caleb and I looked to the side. Sheila had staggered back to the field. I could see her eyes so clearly. They were clouded from the hit she'd taken, but the fire of her soul was trying to push through. She wasn't at full strength, but she'd give all she had. She always would.

I could feel the crackle in the air and the smell of ozone. Her eyes started to glow. And I could hear her—very faintly but clearly enough.

Wait...

Caleb grunted and took a step toward her, still tugging on Orson's jaws. Sheila didn't budge, electricity sparking between her fingers. Caleb feinted at me and juked to Sheila. Orson was still flailing, but Caleb's grip had loosened. Orson squirmed and scratched, finally getting his lower jaw free enough to clamp down on Caleb's thumb. He howled in pain.

Now!

I ran toward him as he shook off Orson, who thumped down into the snow but sprang up again. Sheila swung her arms, sending waves of energy at Caleb, rocking him on his heels.

Smiling, I flipped the claw in my hand. It felt primal and alive. Somewhere, in the recesses of my mind, I remembered something Sheila had once told me about killing. It was quickly washed away on a tide of ice.

Caleb swiveled his head to stare me down with his black eyes. He screamed as Orson bit down hard on his leg. He struggled up, and with a mighty effort, he bellowed in rage and gave a roundhouse kick with the leg Orson was attached to. The dog sailed through the air like a football and crashed into Sheila. Caleb laughed and turned to give me his full attention. Just the two of us.

Good.

I charged at him, blade in hand. He raked his claws at me, but I was ready. I slid underneath his talons, and he tore through nothing but air. On the slide past, I swiped at his leg, aiming for the hamstring behind the knee. A spray of black blood told me I'd struck something. The shriek and thump of Caleb hitting the ground said something too.

Time to finish this.

I sprang up. As if he could sense what was about to happen, Caleb growled like a wounded, trapped animal. I flipped the claw in my hand and approached him as he tried to scrabble to his feet. He tried a desperate lunge at me, but he couldn't get any power off his bad leg, so it was more like a shuffled step. I grabbed his wrist and pulled him forward, stabbing him in the side as he went past me to the ground.

He howled, and it was my turn to laugh. The sound was a deep gurgling, more like the noises of a dying thing in my throat than a sound of pleasure.

Caleb rolled up and took a wild swipe at me. I dodged it easily and went in for the kill. Something tugged at the back of my mind, but I swatted it away like an annoying fly. Sheila was shouting something, but I didn't think it was important.

I pushed Caleb to the ground then dropped onto his chest. I knocked his hand away and drove the blade up under his chin and into his head. He twitched, shuddered, then stilled. The gleam left his eyes. His body crumpled to the ground, a twisted ruin.

It was done. He was done. But I wasn't. I was still hungry.

THIRTY-FOUR

Caleb was dead, but the stone didn't care. It was still inside me, making me this creature. It didn't know or care that the job was done. It would continue controlling its host.

Hosts.

Orson brayed long and loud. He stomped over to Caleb's corpse to sniff at it. He growled at the body. That sparked a trigger deep in me, in the lizard brain. *No. My kill. Mine.*

I shoved him off and, with a shriek, stretched to my full height. Orson rolled back in the snow and barked a challenge, deep and throaty. A piece of my brain knew what was happening. Some sliver knew that this was the stones making us fight over nothing. A part of me knew that, and the rest didn't care. The chenoo stones were ancient magic; they tapped into something primal and basic that didn't care about rational thought. It just made the thrumming in my ears grow louder and louder until it drowned out every other voice, inside or out. That part of my mind accepted the challenge. All of our friendships and bonds forgotten, we were just two monsters fighting over a kill.

Orson leapt at me, teeth bared. I reared back and punched him hard. He yelped and dropped to the ground. My vision narrowed down to a point where everything blurred out around me. I walked forward, intent on finishing the fight. I swung my hand back, about to rake my claws forward, when my arm caught on something.

I glanced back and saw two women hanging from my wrist, pulling my arm back. They looked familiar, very familiar, but I couldn't place them. They were just an annoyance trying to stop me. I spun and shook them off. They flew back into the snow. I took a step toward them, but a sharp pain in my leg forced me to my knee. Their distraction had given the beast a chance to bite my ankle. I kicked, lashing out, but he held strong.

Out of the corner of my eye, I saw the two women gesturing at each other frantically. The younger one shook her head. The older one pointed at me harshly then loped directly at me. I swung a claw at her, but she slid underneath me and the beast, where I wasn't able to follow.

Then I understood. She wasn't running at me but at the body on the ground behind me. She grabbed something on its chin, planted her foot on its shoulder, and pulled hard. With a squelch, a black claw came free, and the woman held it up triumphantly.

I could feel the blade hum. It sang, and the dark music in my blood answered its call. Something told me that it was dangerous. I needed to get it. I spun and tried to stomp on the thing on my leg to get free. He yelped, and that was all I needed. I broke away and with one stride I was face-to-face with the old woman. She glared at me angrily, thrust the claw forward to keep me away, and screamed at me.

I snorted and sneered. She wasn't about to stop me. I started to swing at her hand, my claws out, but an intense pain made me stop. My back burned, as if someone had shoved a lit torch into me.

I arched my back and screamed, but the pain was still there. I looked down. It was the young woman. Her hands were flat against my back, and they were burning. She looked up, anger, hurt, and concern in her golden eyes. I tried to slap her off, but she ducked my swipe then wrapped herself around me. More contact meant more pain. It was unbearable. My insides were going to burn through my skin. I tried to pull her off, but the mongrel clamped down on one arm, and the old woman grabbed the other. She put the flat of the claw against my forearm and pushed hard, and that caused its own burn.

My skin was so hot, the snow around me started to melt. Steam hissed and billowed around me as I sank to my knees in the snow. I was weak. I struggled against those holding me, but I couldn't shake them. I thrashed and bucked, but they were too strong.

I heard a shriek beside me. The young woman had gotten ahold of the dog, and he was burning as well. I heard a sizzle and smelled burning hair. The dog let go of my arm and flopped around in the snow, but he couldn't shake the woman's grip. And even though my arm was freed, it was too weak and damaged to fight them off. It hung by my side.

The heat was unbearable. My lungs felt like they were made of leather, and I couldn't fill them. My ribs contracted around them, binding them tightly. My body was too small. I couldn't fit inside it. I was cramped and trying to stretch, but I couldn't make the tightness go away. The pain drove me to my knees. Gasping, I fell forward and barely held myself up with my hands. Despite the heat coming off my body like flames, I felt cold. So cold.

A wave of nausea overcame me. My body lurched forward. I heaved, but nothing came out. I was choking. I felt a sharp whack on my back between my shoulder blades. Then I vomited up what was blocking my lungs. With a disgusting *horrrck*, a small black rock flew out of my throat. It plopped into the snow, surrounded by a pool of bile.

I gasped. Cold air flooded my lungs. My vision blurred and went black as my strength gave out and I collapsed into the snow.

I WAS BEING SHAKEN. At first, I couldn't tell what was happening. My ears were ringing, but after a few moments, I could make out words. "Come on, wake up!"

Then I felt wetness and heat in my ear, and it drowned her out. Something licked me—and kept on doing it.

Come on, come on. Don't be dead.

It took every ounce of strength to raise my head a quarter of an inch and get my mouth out of the snow. "Sheila? Orson?"

They whooped and cheered. Crying, Sheila hugged me around the neck and shoulders and hauled me up to a sitting position. Orson jumped into my lap and licked my face. Sheila kissed me and held me tight, then she punched me in my chest. Hard.

"You stupid, arrogant..." She ran out of words and smacked me again. "I can't believe you did something like that. And you!" She swatted at Orson. "You just jumped right in as well. You didn't even think if it would hurt you or if you'd be stuck like that."

Orson lowered his head and snuffled in my lap. *But, Mama, you were in trouble.*

"Yeah," I moaned. "Trouble." My head throbbed. Groaning, I scooped up some snow and held it against my temples. It sizzled. My skin was still hot from whatever Sheila had done.

Sheila glared at me. "Serves you right. Bad enough it took all of my energy to fight that deranged monster, then I had to get the two of you back to normal."

But you did it. I knew you would. Orson gave Sheila the sad eyes. It was his tried-and-true method of getting his mama to forgive him for whatever naughty thing he'd done.

She wasn't having it. "Oh no. No. You two swallowed insanely powerful magical stones and turned into monsters. You do *not* get out of this with the sad eyes."

Orson tried to look chastened. I tried my best to look pathetic. It didn't take too much. I barely had the strength to keep from falling over.

"What happened? I remember fighting Caleb, but it all gets a little fuzzy after that."

Sheila frowned. "After the two of you Hulked out, you... Well, it took the both of us, Mona and me, to bring you back."

I helped too!

"Yes, that's right." Sheila scratched his head. "It took everything we had to burn that stone out of you. Orson slowed you down, and Mona used the claw."

As it came back to me, my leg throbbed with the memory. I glanced down and saw blood oozing from two punctures. Orson had bitten me again, but I didn't mind so much this time.

I shivered violently. Sheila's heat was wearing off, and my body remembered that I was sitting in a snowbank in winter. It was then that I realized I was also naked.

"Uh... D-does an-nyone have a b-blanket?"

Mona waggled her eyebrows at me and grinned. "No need to be shy now."

I tried hard to think of something witty, but my teeth were chattering too hard. Fortunately, Sheila and Orson were there to help.

"Ugh, not the time, Mona." Sheila slipped out of her coat and draped it around my shoulders. "If you can stop ogling my fiancé for a minute, go see if there's anything left of his coat that could keep him warm." She pointed to the field, and Mona trudged off, peeking over her shoulder at me.

Sheila leaned in and kissed me softly on the lips. She laid her hand on my chest, and I felt warmth spread through my body. Partly from the magic, partly from the kiss.

Orson got in on the action, planting a sloppy one on my face. *Are we going to have to neuter you?*

"If I spend much longer out here, that's going to be a moot point." Orson licked me again. "Say, how did you get out of beast mode so fast? It took all of you to talk me down from that ledge."

Sheila cradled my head on her shoulder. "Orson's my familiar. You know what a close bond that is and how hard it is to break. It just let me into his head a little easier, and I could get him to calm down and help with you. Plus, his brain is a little simpler than yours."

Orson grunted. *You make it sound like an insult. I just know what I want.*

Usually, that was a cheeseburger.

Sheila scratched his head. "Sorry, baby. I just meant that you are extremely loyal, and it wasn't at all hard to remind you of who you were. Whereas Gabriel"—she punched me fairly softly in the chest—"has a stubborn streak, and it's hard to get him to do anything, even if it's for his own good."

"You should work for Hallmark. That'll make a great Valentine's card."

"It's why I love you. It also drives me crazy."

I was too weak from the fight with Caleb to argue. I let myself slump against her, and my eyes wandered over to the massive thing that used to be Caleb. It wasn't much of anything anymore. Except dead.

"Did I do that? I don't remember a whole lot."

She nodded.

I shivered. Not from the cold. It wasn't the first time I'd killed a man. I'd served in Iraq. I couldn't quote a number, since we didn't take exact counts after a mortar went off in an insurgent stronghold. This time, though, I was up close and personal. And even though I hadn't exactly been myself, I still had to admit I'd killed him. And this time, it was different. I had enjoyed it.

Caleb had been a destructive zealot bent on causing immeasurable pain and suffering. I would just keep telling myself that I hadn't felt a jolt of electricity when I shoved that claw into his brain.

I held myself tight and shook. Sheila held me close and cooed over me. If she could read what I was thinking, she was nice enough not to let on.

THIRTY-FIVE

A few minutes later, Mona trudged back with Rett and Rebecca in tow.

Rett saw the carnage and let out a low whistle. "Damn, son! You don't play, do you?" He nudged the body of the Caleb monster with his foot. "He didn't turn back?"

Sheila shook her head. "I guess that as long as the stone is in him, it'll keep working."

I gasped and touched my side. I felt for the wound where Caleb had stabbed me. It was sore but still patched up. "Can you get the stone out of him?"

Sheila was puzzled. "Why?"

"When I was... different, Caleb stabbed me with the claw, but the stone healed me once it was out." I looked over and saw the hole in his chin where I'd shoved that claw. "I don't know how strong that magic is, but I don't want to be around if it resurrects him. "

Mona looked at the wound and looked at the body. "It shouldn't be too hard. I think the one in your body kind of latched on to your energy, and that's why it was so hard to get out of you. There's nothing in him to hang on to, and any magic in the stone is keeping that corpse intact."

She held her hand over Caleb's remains. The air hummed as she concentrated. Heat shimmered in the space between her palm and his chest. After a moment, a tiny bulge appeared in his stomach. It pulled toward Mona's hand, stretching at the taut skin until, finally, it popped out like a cork, tearing through the skin. It hovered under her hand. It looked as black and broken as the one that had come out of me.

Good thing we let you puke yours up, huh? Orson, master of understatement.

Once the stone was out, Caleb shrank like a deflating balloon. The limbs and torso didn't quite make it back to their old dimensions, and he reminded me of an old chew toy that Orson had discarded after loving it too much.

Mona dropped the stone she'd pulled out of Caleb next to the one I'd puked up. They looked harmless, but I wasn't about to touch them.

I glanced back at Rebecca and Rett. "What happened to the others?"

Rebecca was staring at the body, looking a little shell-shocked, which was understandable. The man she'd once pledged her loyalty to had become a literal monster and was now lying in a crumpled heap.

Rett jumped in and spoke up. "The ones we didn't knock out ran away when they saw Caleb..." He pointed at the body. "Anyway, we'd better get out of here too. No telling if they went to get help."

Sheila agreed. "Yes, time to go. Gabe, are you able to walk?"

I nodded. "Sure." I staggered to my feet then immediately got dizzy and fell face-first into the snow. "Uh. Maybe not." I was keenly aware of a breeze tickling my butt, but I was too exhausted to do much about it.

Rett and Sheila jumped forward.

"Come on, kid. Let's sit you up." Rett repositioned me so that he and Sheila could lift me across their shoulders and get me out of there. They went as fast as they could, dragging my exhausted body back to the camper.

We left as fast as we dared. As we passed the gates to the remains of the plant, I could still see the TV trucks out front, but the ride back to town was uneventful. Thank goodness.

We sat in Rett's trailer in silence. He'd found me a pair of sweats to change into. I was still exhausted, and I dozed off several times. Every time the camper hit a pothole, though, it jolted me awake.

When we arrived at the garage where I'd left the Galaxie, I could still barely move, so Sheila went in to deal with the mechanic. Through the window, I could see her smiling and chatting with the guy. He smiled back and gave her the keys. Sheila brushed his arm and laughed. Then she walked out to our car, started it up, and drove off. The mechanic waved at her happily.

Orson woofed. *So is he my new daddy now?*

"Stop it." I moaned.

Bet he's good with his hands.

"I'm sure Sheila just charmed him so he'd forget about loaning us that car that got squashed."

Right.

Rett followed Sheila a few blocks away until she pulled into the parking lot of a Walmart, where I shuffled out of the camper and into the passenger seat of my car. Orson scrambled after me and jumped onto my lap.

"So," I asked, "should I be jealous?"

"Yep. He promised me discounts on winter tires. A girl just can't turn down an offer like that."

Knew it.

"Oh hush, Orson. I just made him agreeable to not charging us for the car Caleb trashed out by Mona's. He has insurance. Plus, he gave me a sweetheart deal on the axle. Just charged me for parts."

"I wonder what made him have such a kind heart?"

Sheila smiled. "'Tis a mystery." She tried to wrinkle her nose *Bewitched*-style.

"You look like you're trying not to sneeze, Samantha."

"Hey!"

I leaned in to kiss her. "It's adorable."

"That's better, Darrin."

She shifted into gear and drove off into the late afternoon sun, which was just starting to dip into our line of sight. We were going back to the road that would take us toward what used to be Mona's cottage. It had been a long couple of days, and I could barely keep my eyes open. Sheila was doing better than me, but not by much.

I reached over and touched her arm. "Let's stop for a bit, okay? Mona's not going to have a place for us since her house is demolished, and I really do not want to sleep in the camper."

She leaned her head to me, a tired grin on her face. "Sounds good." She took a left at the next light and headed off to the motel we'd stayed at before the bear forced us out.

The manager remembered us—it was hard to forget a thing like that—and offered us a complimentary room for the night. We promised him a good Yelp review. Everybody won.

Once inside the room, we all collapsed on the bed and stared at the ceiling. There was a water stain up there that looked a lot like Godzilla. It was fascinating. I imagined the water stain rampaging through Tokyo as I fell into a deep and dreamless sleep.

THIRTY-SIX

I pried open my eyes. It took some doing, as my eye goop had made a crust and sealed them shut. With some effort, I got a look at the clock radio on the side table. 9:23. In the morning, I guessed, based on the wan light peeking through the curtains. I did the math in my head as quickly as I was able to. I'd been out for a good sixteen hours.

I rolled over to see if Sheila was still asleep, but her side of the bed was empty. I didn't see Orson, either. They must've gone out for a walk and let me sleep. I sat up and felt sixteen hours of pee slosh in my bladder. I lurched out of bed and staggered to the bathroom.

As I finished up, I heard the door click open. I poked my head out of the bathroom, and I was relieved to see Sheila, with Orson bounding ahead of her. He leapt onto the bed then launched himself at me.

You're alive! He hit me square in the chest. It took all my strength not to fall back into the toilet.

"Yeah, buddy. I am! Try not to sound too relieved."

Orson ignored me and licked my face repeatedly.

Sheila extricated Orson from me. "We were a little worried. You were asleep and dead to the world for a while."

I yawned. "I know. I don't think I've slept sixteen hours in a while. Maybe after I had a bender when I got back from overseas..."

Sheila glanced at Orson and stared at me. "Um, try sixteen hours plus another twenty-four. We checked in here on Tuesday afternoon. It's Thursday morning now."

That made me tired all over again, and I slumped down on the edge of the bed. My stomach growled loudly. Sheila grabbed a McDonald's bag from the bureau and sat down next to me.

"Here, eat this."

I found two McGriddles inside the bag.

"I got these for Orson and me, but we can make a trip back for more."

Orson whined from the floor.

"Enough! It's not like you didn't scarf two down yesterday. You're just lucky I'm a softie."

He sleeps all day, and *he steals my food?*

Sheila smirked at him. "I guess dogs don't grasp the concept of irony. C'mon, sweetie, let Gabe eat in peace."

She kissed me on the cheek then gestured to a bag on a chair in the corner. "We got you some new clothes at the Walmart. Since, you know..." She hugged me gently then led Orson away. He glared at me as they walked outside.

I sighed. I took a bite of the first sandwich, and before I even realized it, I was wadding up the wrappers of both of them. I could barely recall swallowing, let alone tasting. I guess Caleb really had done a number on me.

My eyes widened. *Oh yeah. We... I kinda murdered a guy. Maybe we shouldn't be hanging around here.* I turned on the TV and scanned the channels. Nothing but game shows and morning talk. The local news break at the end of *The Today Show* was based out of Bangor and just mentioned the weather. No mention of a murdered, misshapen body found in the woods by the pulp mill wreckage. So there was that, at least.

Even though the room was warm, I shivered. Sheila always said the bad things we do left marks on us. I'd done plenty of bad things in my life. I wondered how marked up I already was. Was this the thing that cursed me forever?

At that moment, Sheila returned. She had another sack of take-out food and a tray of coffee. Orson jumped up on the bed next to me while Sheila put the food down and shrugged off her coat. "I thought you might still be hungry." She saw the balled-up wrappers still in my hand. "And what do you know!" She tossed me a bundle of greasy goodness. "And when don't you want coffee?" She handed me the cup and smiled kindly as our fingers touched.

"You know me so well."

She brushed my cheek with her fingers. "Yes." She looked away for a second. "I couldn't help but overhear you when I came in. I know you hate that, and I'm really trying to stop it, but it just happened."

I closed my eyes and sipped the scalding coffee.

"I didn't want you and Orson to do that," Sheila said. "It was dangerous, and you both could have died. But I'm glad you did."

I opened my eyes to glance at her. The amber flecks in her eyes glowed as she looked deep into mine. "It took all of us to beat him. I couldn't have done it myself." I started to open my mouth, but she put a finger on my lips. "Stop. You will never be too damaged for me. You may have taken on the form of a monster, but it was only to save me. Your heart and your spirit, that was all Gabriel."

I dropped the sandwich on the bed and held her close. "Thank you."

It was such a relief to hear, a tear ran down my cheek and onto her shoulder. She hugged me so tightly, I barely noticed Orson gobbling up my sandwich.

What? It's no good cold.

AFTER WE'D FINISHED our coffee and eaten the sandwiches that Orson had left for us, we checked out. Sheila wanted to drop in on Mona before we headed off to... Well, I wasn't quite sure where we were going.

After the short drive, we bounced down the road to the remains of Mona's cottage. It looked even worse in the light of day than I remembered. The red Neon with the crumpled front was still there, as was the tree that Sheila had dropped on Caleb. Rett's camper was there as well. As we pulled up, Mona flung open the door and jumped down to meet us.

"Glad you two could make it!" As I hauled myself out of the driver's seat, Mona clamped me in a bear hug. "I was worried about you! Sheila said you were tough, but I was still worried." She gave me a big kiss before she let me go. She turned to Sheila and gave her a much gentler embrace. "I know *you're* tough. Tougher than me, for sure."

Rett jumped down next and gave me a big slap on the back that nearly knocked me over. "Welcome back, kid!"

"Thanks. Careful, you'll knock me back into a mini coma."

He laughed at that but still whacked my back again.

I looked back at the camper. "Is Rebecca in there?"

He shook his head. "We drove her down to the bus station. She's going to head back down to Portland, try and get back into school." He grinned and shrugged. "I guess she's had enough of the real-life environmental battles for now."

Mona had drifted away from the camper over to the edge of the field that once held her home. Sheila slid up next to her and laced her fingers with Mona's.

"I'm so sorry about this. You asked us to help, and I made a mess of everything."

Mona clucked her tongue. "Nonsense. Things were already a mess. You just helped to... sweep away the clutter."

"That's one word for it." Sheila kicked at a bit of rubble by her foot. "What are you going to do now?"

Mona sighed. "I've been here for years. I tried to settle down, relax, do the 'retiree' thing, but no luck. Truth be told, it was getting a little dull. So I think I'll head out with Rett for a while. There's still a lot of work to be done, and it's nice to have someone around to talk to."

Rett came over to drape his arms around her. "Yeah, she's going to ride with me until she gets sick of me. That should be at least a week."

Mona rolled her eyes. "It took way longer than that last time. Like two weeks. And I promise not to nuke anything this time."

Orson and I made our way over. "When are you heading out?" I asked.

Rett cricked his neck. "No reason to stick around. Mona got every-thing she could out of the house. We were mainly waiting to make sure you were okay. So we'll get moving as soon as she wants."

"Then I'd better do this now." I reached out to Mona and took her hand. "Can you do something for us, before you leave?"

Mona was surprised, and so was Sheila. "Sure. What is it, dearie?"

"You're a priestess, right?"

"Yes, but I haven't done anything with it in a while. Why do you—"

"Can you marry us?"

THIRTY-SEVEN

Sheila gasped, and I turned to her to explain myself. "I'm sorry to surprise you, but after everything we've been through this week, I don't want to wait a second longer."

Sheila took my hand gently and brought it up to her face. "I know you hate when I hear what you're thinking. I honestly had no idea."

Me, neither. Orson rubbed his head on my leg.

I brushed her soft cheek with my fingers. "We almost lost each other again." I brought her in close for a kiss. "Not another time. We're in this together. For always."

Mona approached us. "I'm happy to do the ceremony—that is, if Sheila wants me to."

Sheila flung her arms around my neck and hugged me. "Of course. Of course I do. I was starting to wonder if this was going to happen."

Mona giggled. "About time. Now, let's see what we can whip up."

Mona rooted around the rubble of her cottage, and Rett jumped into the camper. After a few minutes, they came back with their finds.

"It's been a while since I did a handfasting," Mona said. "And most of my supplies aren't usable. So we'll have to improvise." She shifted her hands to adjust her load. "Now, usually we need a ribbon or cord to tie your hands together. We need a cake and a ceremonial dagger and some mead in a chalice. And we need a broom."

"Uh... Why? Sorry, I just didn't know it would be so involved."

Mona raised an eyebrow. "There are no shortcuts in wedding rituals, young man. The cord is used to tie your and Sheila's hands together. This symbolizes you being tied together in life."

I nodded like I was a smart person. "Sure."

"At the end of the ceremony, you two leap over the broom. This is a symbolic leap over the threshold of your new home together."

"Right, I've heard of that."

Mona continued. "And the ritual of the cakes and ale, well, that symbolizes the combining of the god and the goddess. The dagger, or athame—the male element—gets plunged into the chalice of mead, the female element. Once they are combined, the dagger is used to cut the cake as a symbol of fertility."

You had me at cake.

Mona scratched Orson on the ear. "I bet I did, sweetie. Anyway, we had to improvise a little."

Rett proudly held up a red plastic cup, a bottle of beer, and a plastic-wrapped snack cake. "No mead, but I had some Yuengling in the car! And a Tastykake Butterscotch Krimpet. Best cake in the world!"

Mona held up a nail file. "No dagger, but this will do! And look!" She proudly displayed a small whisk. "I found my little hand broom, so we got that covered."

I looked at her props. "So I guess we just need a cord or a string."

Mona looked down. "Yeah, no luck with that. I could even use a shoelace, but I'm wearing slip-ons."

Sheila put her hands behind her neck and unclasped her silver crescent moon necklace. "We'll use this."

The necklace was one of the first things I'd ever bought her. I got it from a vendor outside the Met museum, and she wore it all the time. It had recently been used by a creep as a way to tell me she was being held hostage. Once I'd gotten her out of there, I was only too happy to put it back on her.

"Sounds good to me!" Mona took the necklace. "No time like the present! Let's get started."

SO THAT WAS HOW WE wound up calf deep in snow, being married by a monk and a wiccan priestess, with a bulldog for a best man. It was almost exactly like I'd dreamed when I was a boy except that Sheila was way prettier than Cindy Crawford.

Mona stood near the ruined cottage with Rett by her side to help officiate. I could barely hear her speaking. Even though it had been my idea, I couldn't believe it was happening. I hadn't thought it would be such a big deal to me. We'd been living together for a while. We were essentially married already. But with Mona and Rett standing in front of me with all of the ceremonial props, it suddenly felt special and momentous.

Sheila grinned at me happily. Mona had managed to scavenge a few twigs and flowers from the wreath on her door and fashion Sheila a woodsy tiara. It was a fitting crown for my lady.

The ceremony was a bit of a blur. Mona was invoking the goddess, and Rett was invoking the Christian God, but all I could see was Sheila's beautiful face. It had been years since Orson and Sheila had literally run into me in the park. We'd been through a lot since then, and I couldn't wait for more.

My thoughts and heart were so full of Sheila that the ceremony became more of an undercurrent in the background, like the trickle of a spring brook, with a few words breaking through the surface now and then.

"... joined together... eyes of the Goddess... aspects of both..."

Rett offered the Solo cup of Philadelphian ale. Mona wrapped Sheila's hand and mine around the handle of the nail file. "We join together the athame and chalice as we join you two in love, a union of spirit and soul." Mona guided our hand to the cup and plunged the file in. I felt a jolt run up to our hands and down my arm. Sheila let out a sharp breath.

Mona then moved our athame-slash-salon tool to the unwrapped butterscotch krimpet, jauntily displayed on a paper plate. "And may this union be blessed with a bountiful harvest and want for nothing." The athame dove into the snack cake, and even though it was a beer-coated nail file cutting into a mass-produced pastry, I still felt a shiver of power and energy run through me. Sheila swayed a bit. She'd told me once that love was the strongest magic.

Mona took the blade from us and set it down on the plate, but we still held hands tightly. "And now, you two souls shall be bound as one." She took Sheila's unclasped necklace and started to loosely wrap it around our entwined hands. Mona said a few more words, but I couldn't stop looking at Sheila.

She'd done so much for me. She'd helped me put out all the anger that had burned inside me for decades. She'd taught me what real love was and what real respect was. Some days, I wondered why she'd chosen me and why she put up with me or spent the time and energy to help me mature.

I heard her in my head then. *Gabe, because no one else ever loved me like you.*

I felt a tear run down my cheek.

And your butt is cute. Don't forget that part.

I bit my lip to keep from laughing.

Mona either hadn't heard Sheila or had wisely chosen to ignore her, because she went on without pause. "These are the hands that will care for you. These are the hands that will console you. These are the hands that will hold you close. These are the hands that will wipe away the tears. These are the hands that will start a life together."

Rett joined in to say a blessing over us. "Now you will feel no rain, for each of you will be shelter for the other. Now you will feel no cold, for you will be warmth to the other. Now there will be no loneliness, for each of you will be companion to the other. Now you are two persons, but there are three lives before you—his life, her life, and your life together. Go now to your dwelling place, to enter into the days of your life together."

Sheila's grin warmed my heart, and I heard Orson grunt. *Does he mean the car? Are we going to live in the car?*

I nudged him with my foot. He waddled forward, and with my free hand, I plucked the ring off his collar. I had bought it for Sheila last summer on Virginia Beach when I proposed to her. I hadn't found a nicer one for a wedding band, so it would have to do.

Mona looked at me. "Do you take Sheila, to love and to cherish, to care for and to protect, and to be your wife?"

I nodded, barely able to speak. "Yes. I do."

She looked to Sheila. "And Sheila, do you take Gabriel, to love and to cherish, to care for and to protect, and to be your husband?"

Her smile was so big, it looked like it would split her face. "Yes! I do. I do!"

I slipped the ring onto her finger.

"Then by the powers of the god and the goddess, and the Unitarian Universalist Church, I declare you to be husband and wife."

Sheila leapt into my arms, a bit of a tricky thing considering that two of our hands were still tied together. She wrapped her free arm around my neck, and I scooped her up with mine.

She kissed me hard then whispered in my ear, "I love you."

"I love you," I whispered back.

She giggled. "I set you up for a Star Wars joke, and you turned it down? Who are you?"

"Just a lucky nerf herder."

While we'd been kissing, Mona had laid the tiny hand broom at our feet. "Now you may start your life's journey together."

I turned away from the altar and, with an awkward hop, leapt over the broom and into the future. It was official. We were married.

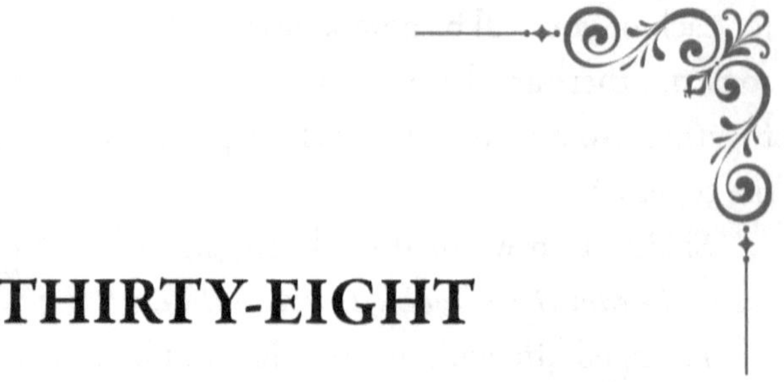

THIRTY-EIGHT

We didn't have much of a reception. We shared the few beers and Tastykakes that Rett had in the camper, but it was already starting to get dark. We had cramped around the camper table, eating the last bits of snack food.

"I didn't realize you were a Unitarian, Mona," I said.

"Oh. That's just for the legal parts of the marriages. I ordered that 'officiant' card in a catalog a long time ago. Just makes it easier with certain counties and officials that think Pagan means 'Satanist.' So you're legal in all fifty states." She gave me a sheet of paper that she and Rett had both signed. "Signed and witnessed. All official and everything."

Sheila took Mona's hand. "Thank you for this. I had no idea he was going to do it. Did you?"

Mona looked me over. "I knew he would. Just wasn't sure about the when. I'm glad I could be here, though."

I'm glad there's cake. Orson chewed noisily then licked up the last few crumbs.

I turned to Rett, who was pouring out the last of his Yeungling. "Where to now?"

Rett shrugged. "Well, hopefully, there's an environmental crisis somewhere warmer. I'm happy to go where I'm called, but maybe we could picket a beach in San Diego or something. I hear there's one that the seals have taken over. Maybe we can go have a lie-in with them."

Mona hooted. "Sounds good to me! I haven't been out west in ages. How about you two?"

Sheila rubbed her shoulders. "I'm with Rett. Time to go look for magical monsters in warmer places."

No more monsters. Just cake.

I scratched Orson's ears. "We promise cake. We'll do our best on the monsters."

NOT LONG AFTER THAT, we drove off. We headed down to Houlton. In the morning, we would move south, off to someplace warm. We would let Wendy in Florida know how things turned out.

But first, our honeymoon. In snowy, frosty Maine.

We found a place that met Orson's exacting demands of a breakfast buffet with waffles and HBO in the room. And because it was our honeymoon and all, I splurged on a name-brand hotel where we didn't park in front of the room. Then we ordered the finest selections room service had to offer, which was from the local pizza place that had an ad on the hotel key card. We toasted with plastic cups full of Diet Coke and enjoyed our pepperoni-and-green-pepper slices. Orson begged piteously until we gave him a slice. He gobbled it up then promptly fell asleep in a cheese coma. He snored loudly. As always.

Sheila snuggled up to me in bed. "Hello, husband."

"Hello, wife."

"I like how that sounds."

"Me too." I stroked her hair. "Hey, remember what Mona said, about how the cakes-and-ale ritual was a fertility blessing?"

"Yeah, so? I mean 'honeymoon' literally means the month you drink mead because it's supposed to make you more fertile."

"Should I go get some condoms?"

I felt her chuckle into my chest. "It might be a little late for that."

I sat up in bed. "What?"

She looked down at her lap a bit sheepishly. "I was going to tell you back at Wendy's place, but, well, things took a turn."

"Are you... did you take a test?"

She nodded.

I looked at Orson, who was still snoring off his pizza on the floor. "Is this what Orson meant? He told me you were worried about something but wouldn't say what."

"It probably was. It's so sweet of him to be concerned. Are you okay, Gabe?"

I was stunned. I'd never dreamed I would be a father. My parents were such awful examples that I could never imagine inflicting that on a kid of my own. But only a few years ago, I couldn't have imagined someone like Sheila, either.

I hugged her to me tightly. My breath came out in a sob. "Yes. Yes, I'm fine. I've never been better."

I kissed her and felt something hard inside of me melt. We had been through a lot together, and this promised much more to come. The honeymoon had just begun.

Acknowledgements

There are so many people to thank. First, thank you to my amazing editors, Sara and Stefanie, who took my ramblings and made them into a coherent story where people aren't repeatedly smiling at each other and nodding.

Thanks to my Mom and Detta and the others in their reading group who would prod me for the latest chapter and send encouragement.

Thanks to all my writing friends who offer encouragement and support on the days I would rather be doing self-dentistry than write any more words: Karissa Laurel, Katrina Monroe, Jaime Leigh, Mary Fan, Kate Birdsall, Scott Bell, and Kelley Kaye. They're all great writers. Look them up and buy all their stuff!

And most of all, thank you to all the fans who bought *Tail and Trouble*. The response was amazing. Special thanks to the nice reviewer who baked Orson cookies. It's great to know there are people out there who like what I do.

Please feel free to leave a review on Goodreads or Amazon or your favorite book site to let others know how you felt about my book. It really helps to get the word out.

And to keep up to date on all things Orson related, follow me on social media. I love to hear from you. Plus there are lots of pictures of Dany the Pughuaua, so wins all around.

About the Author

Victor Catano lives in New York City with his wonderful wife, Kim, and their adorable pughuaua, Danerys. When not writing, he works in live theater as a stage manager, light designer, and production manager.

His hobbies include coffee, Broadway musicals, and complaining about the NY Mets and Philadelphia Eagles.

Read more at https://VictorCatanoAuthor.weebly.com.

About the Publisher

Dear Reader,

We hope you enjoyed this book. Please consider leaving a review on your favorite book site.

Visit https://RedAdeptPublishing.com to see our entire catalogue.

Don't forget to subscribe to our monthly newsletter to be notified of future releases and special sales.

www.ingramcontent.com/pod-product-compliance
Lightning Source LLC
Chambersburg PA
CBHW050400190726
48284CB00007BB/2371